S0-BCM-457

SUPER POWERS!

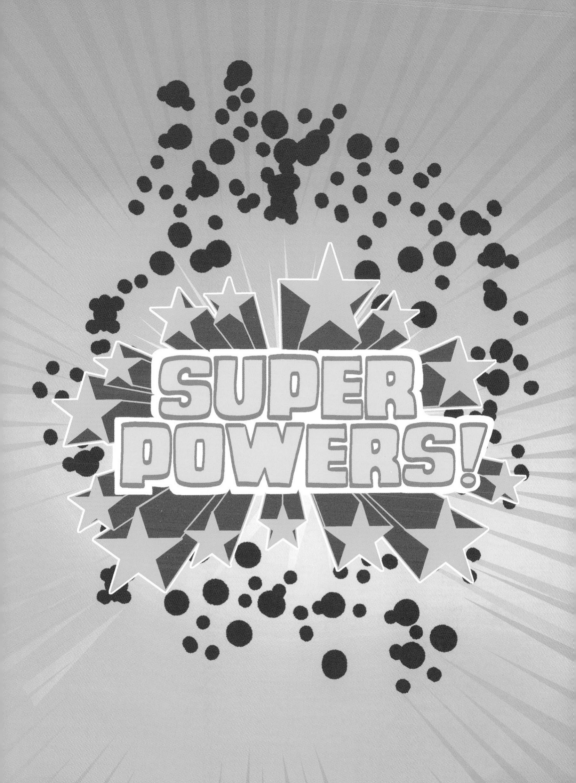

Super Powers! is published by
Stone Arch Books,
A Capstone Imprint
1710 Roe Crest Drive
North Mankato, Minnesota 56003
www.mycapstone.com

Cataloging-in-Publication Data is available at the Library of Congress website:
ISBN: 978-1-4965-7395-7 (library binding)
ISBN 978-1-4965-7401-5 (eBook PDF)

Summary: Batman has been kidnapped! As Brainiac holds him captive on New Krypton, Superman and Wonder Woman rush to save him. But someone else is lurking behind this evil plot . . .

Printed in the United States.
PA021

STONE ARCH BOOKS
Chris Harbo Editorial Director
Gena Chester Editor
Hilary Wacholz Art Director
Kris Wilfahrt Production Specialist

Superman created by Jerry Siegel and Joe Shuster. By special arrangement with the Jerry Siegel family.

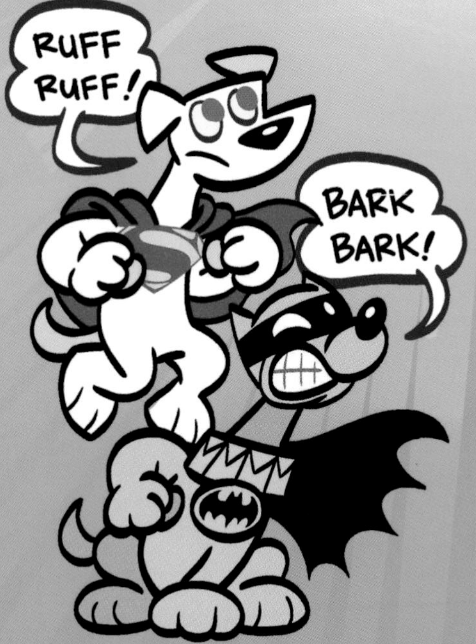
RUFF RUFF!
BARK BARK!

SUPER POWERS!

Dark Knight Dilemma!

BY ART BALTAZAR AND FRANCO

STONE ARCH BOOKS
a capstone imprint

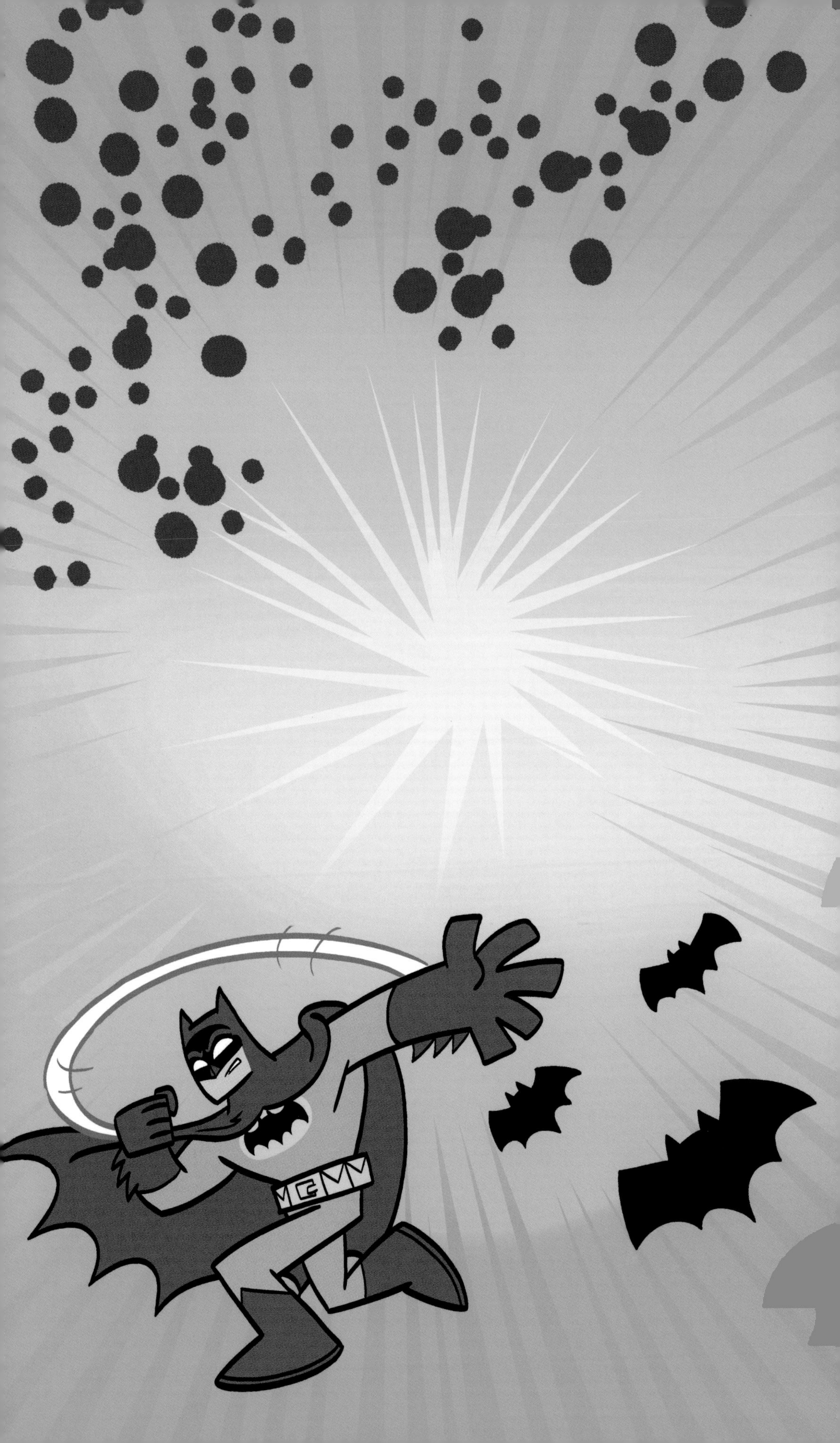

DC COMICS PROUDLY PRESENTS...

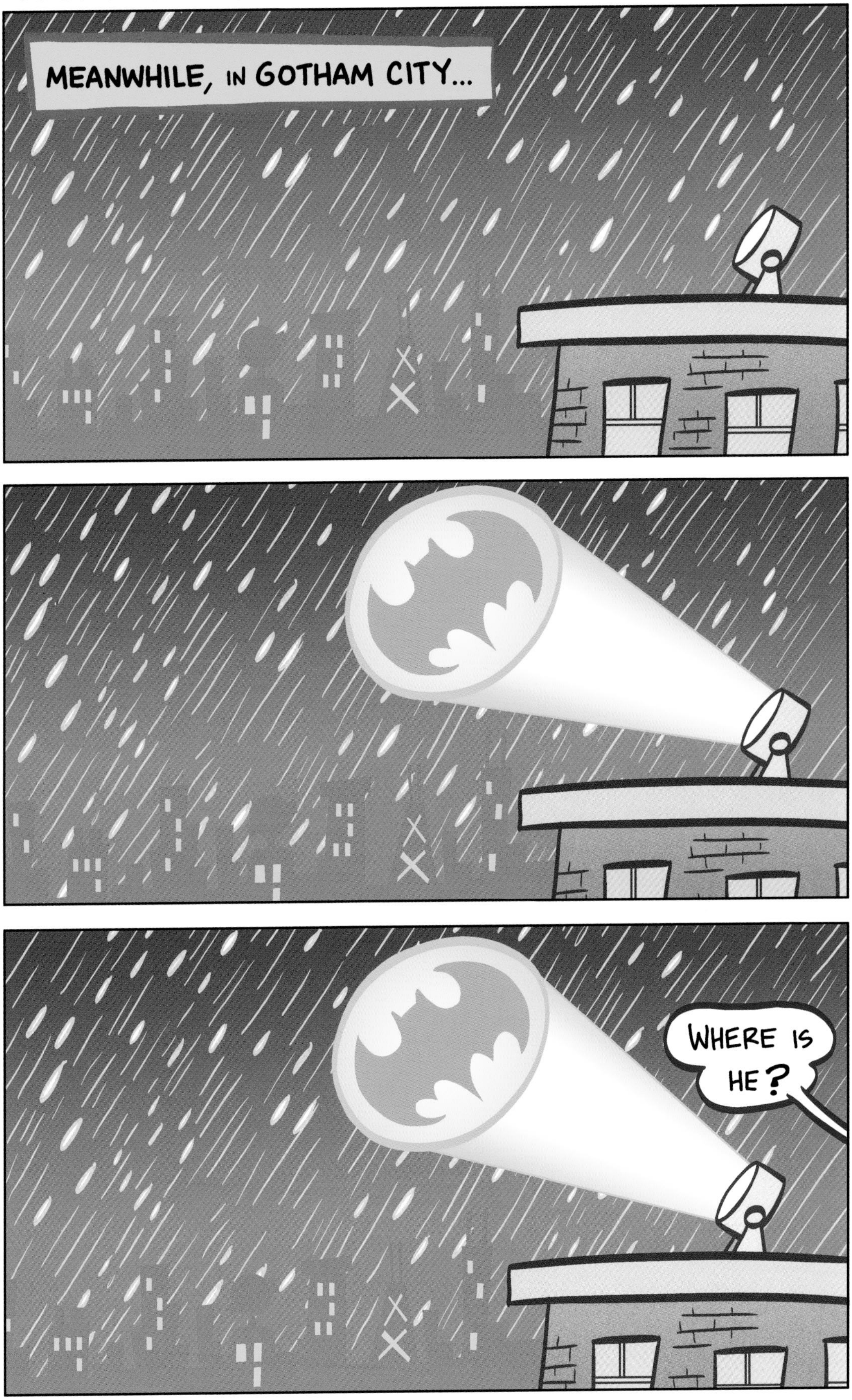
MEANWHILE, IN GOTHAM CITY...
WHERE IS HE?

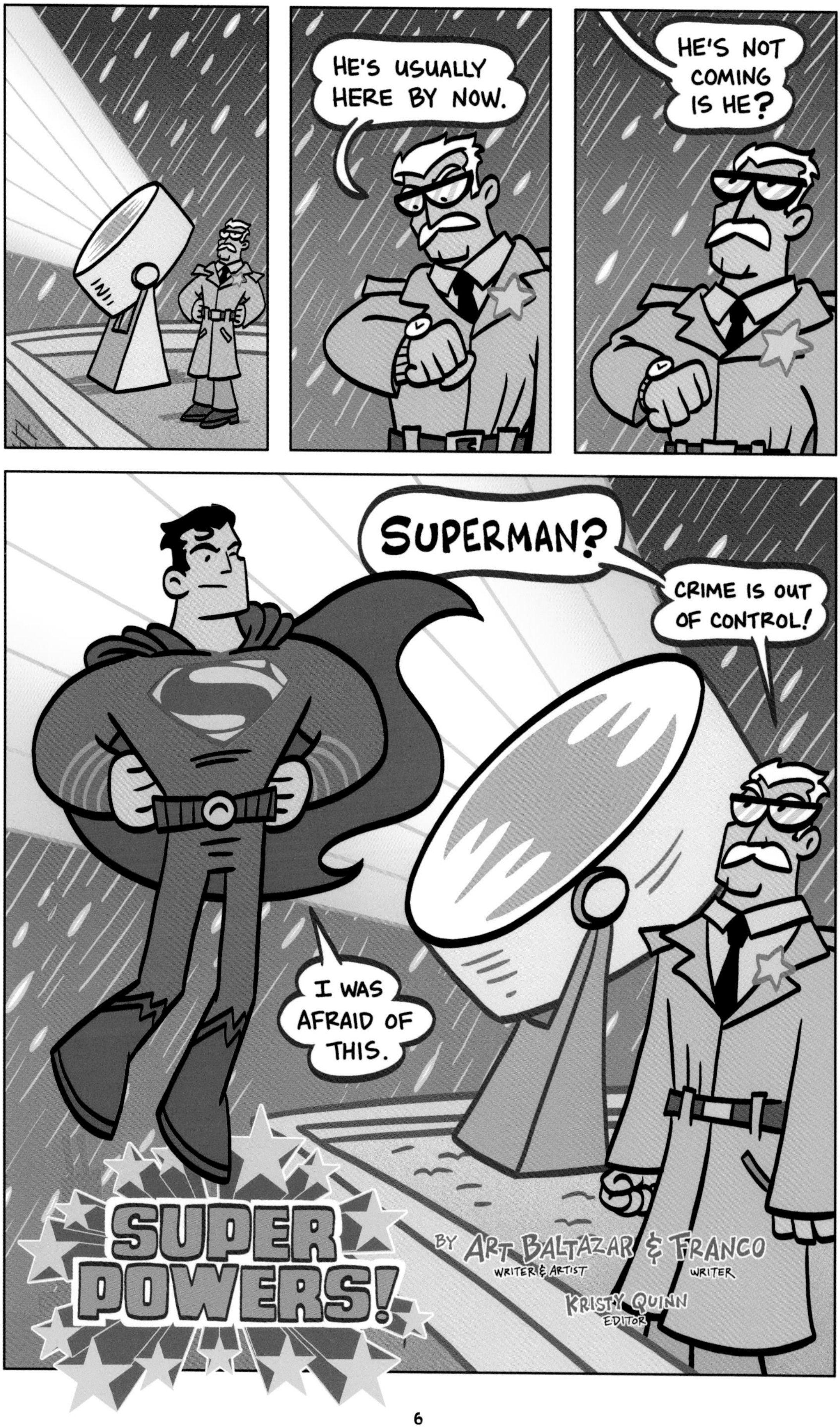
HE'S USUALLY HERE BY NOW.
HE'S NOT COMING IS HE?
SUPERMAN?
CRIME IS OUT OF CONTROL!
I WAS AFRAID OF THIS.
SUPER POWERS!
BY ART BALTAZAR WRITER & ARTIST & FRANCO WRITER
KRISTY QUINN EDITOR

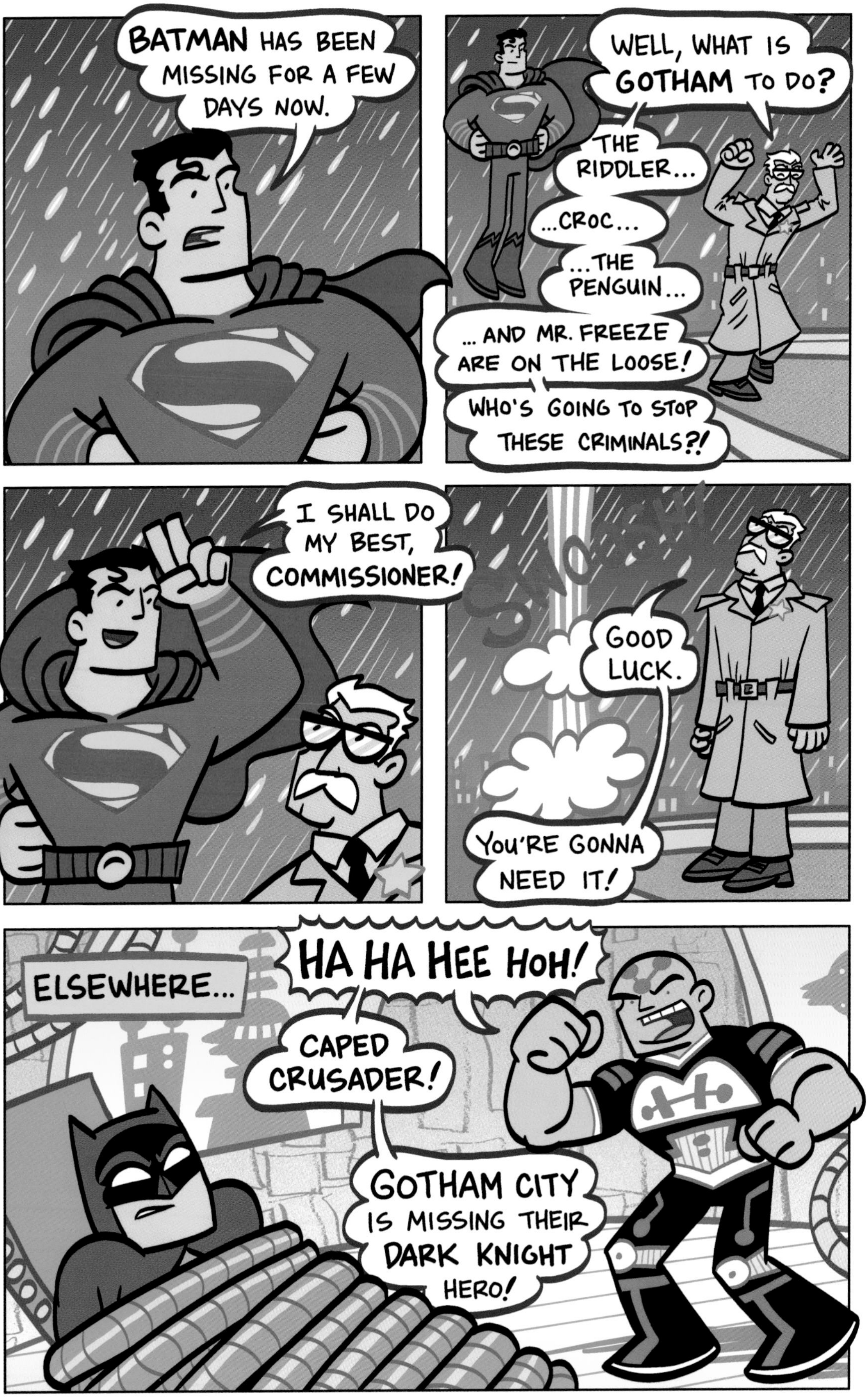
BATMAN HAS BEEN MISSING FOR A FEW DAYS NOW.
WELL, WHAT IS GOTHAM TO DO?
THE RIDDLER...
...CROC...
...THE PENGUIN...
... AND MR. FREEZE ARE ON THE LOOSE!
WHO'S GOING TO STOP THESE CRIMINALS?!
I SHALL DO MY BEST, COMMISSIONER!
SWOOSH!
GOOD LUCK.
YOU'RE GONNA NEED IT!
ELSEWHERE...
HA HA HEE HOH!
CAPED CRUSADER!
GOTHAM CITY IS MISSING THEIR DARK KNIGHT HERO!

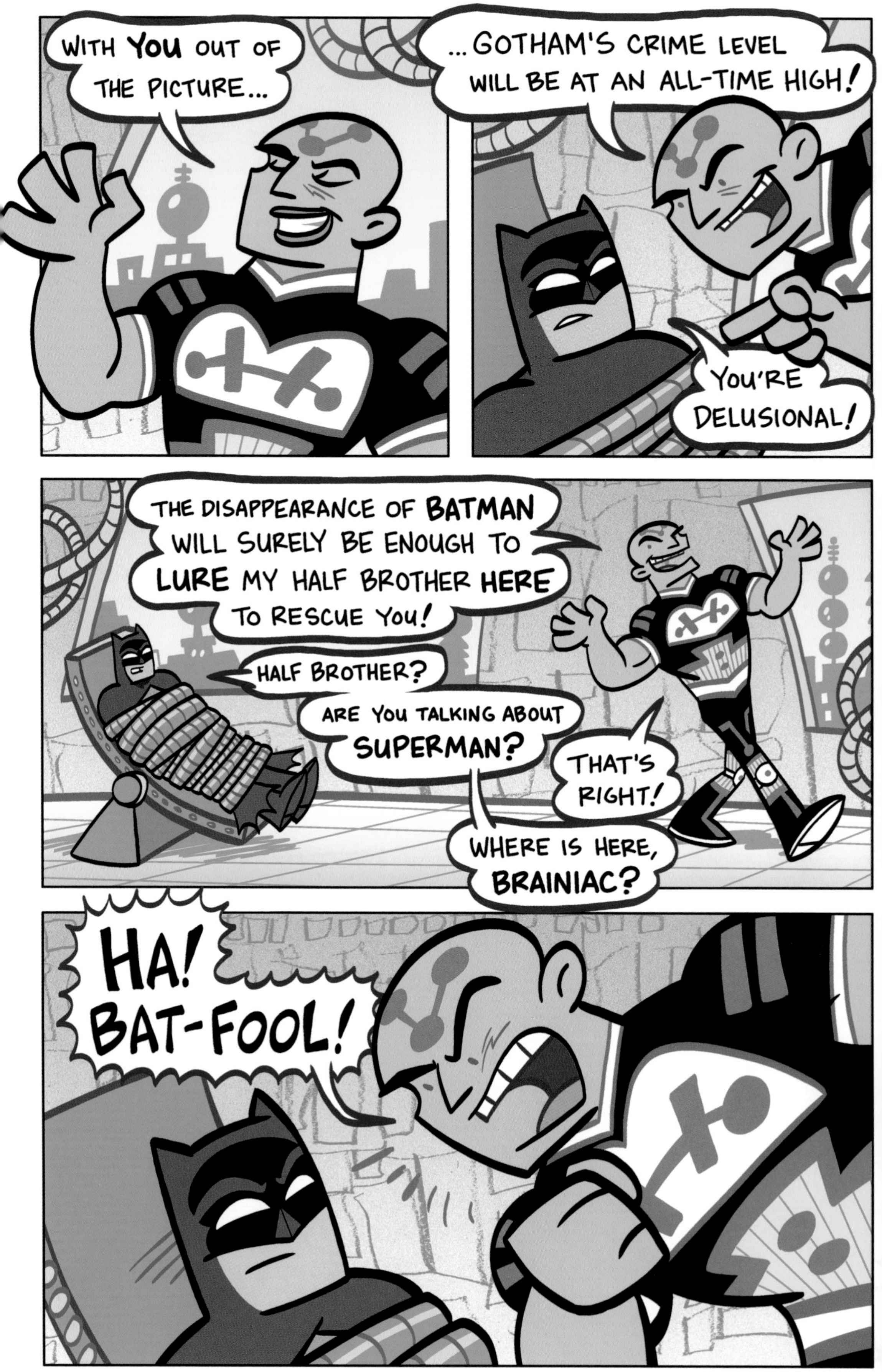
WITH YOU OUT OF THE PICTURE...
...GOTHAM'S CRIME LEVEL WILL BE AT AN ALL-TIME HIGH!
YOU'RE DELUSIONAL!
THE DISAPPEARANCE OF BATMAN WILL SURELY BE ENOUGH TO LURE MY HALF BROTHER HERE TO RESCUE YOU!
HALF BROTHER?
ARE YOU TALKING ABOUT SUPERMAN?
THAT'S RIGHT!
WHERE IS HERE, BRAINIAC?
HA! BAT-FOOL!

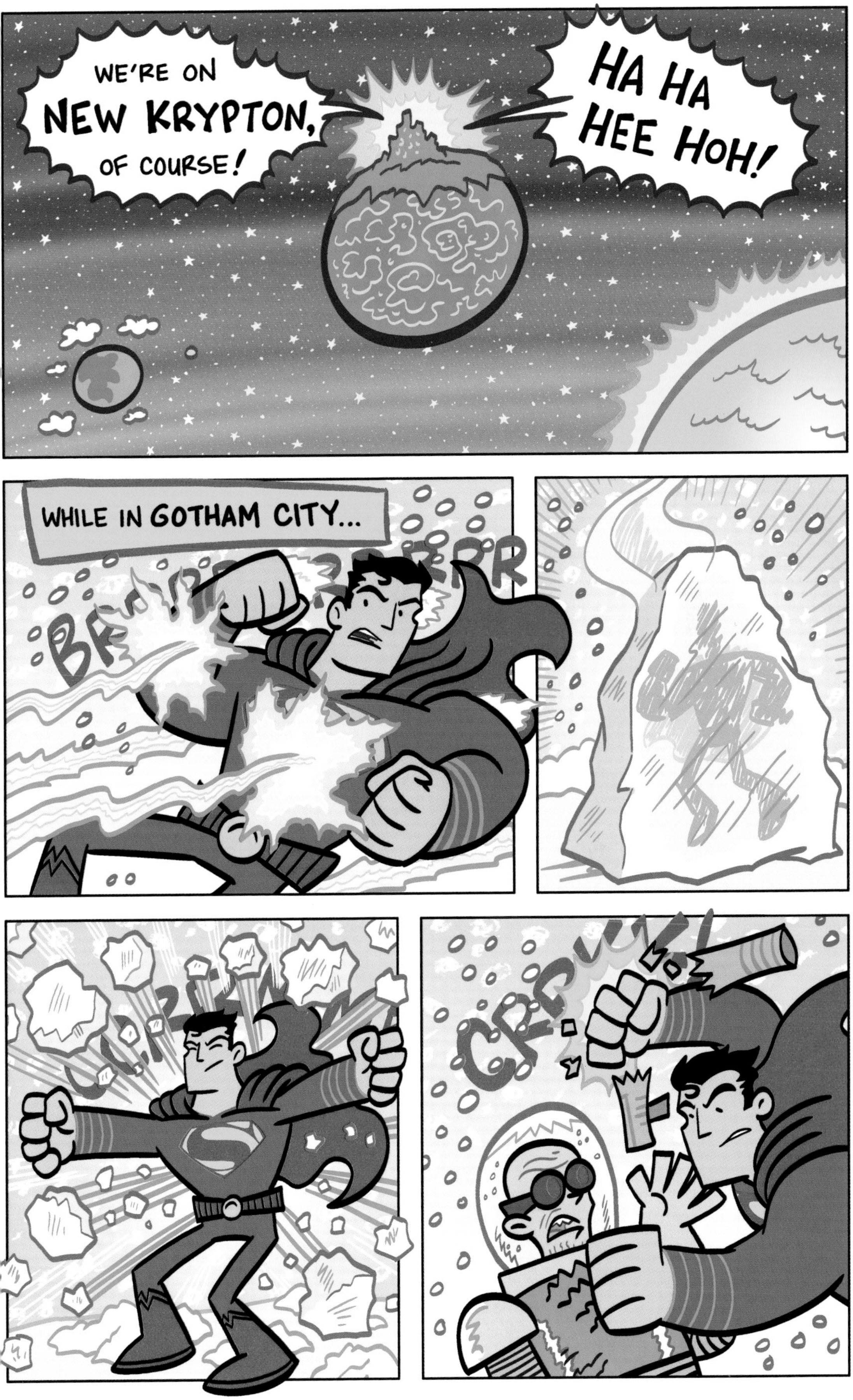
WE'RE ON NEW KRYPTON, OF COURSE!
HA HA HEE HOH!
WHILE IN GOTHAM CITY...

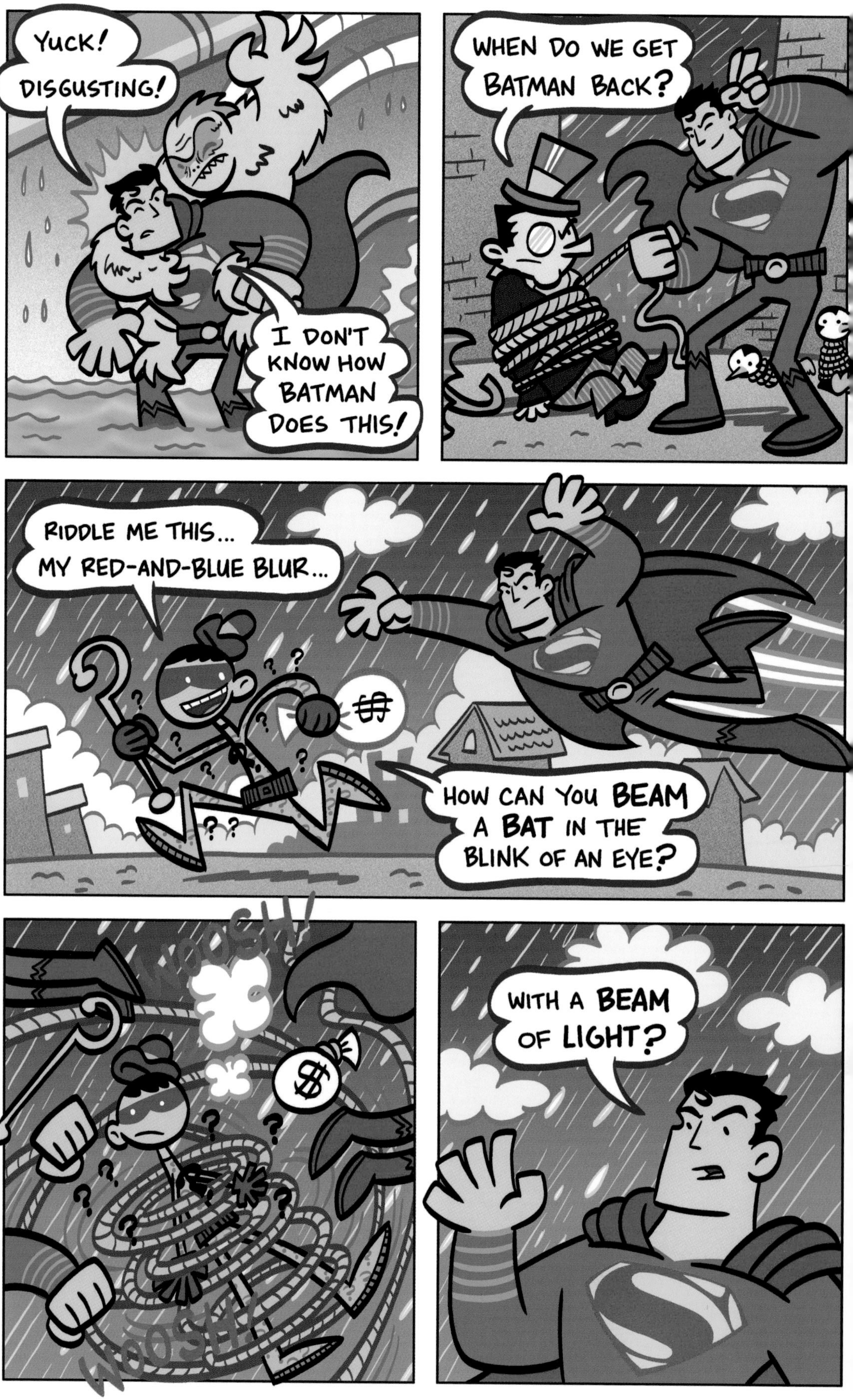
YUCK!
DISGUSTING!
I DON'T KNOW HOW BATMAN DOES THIS!
WHEN DO WE GET BATMAN BACK?
RIDDLE ME THIS... MY RED-AND-BLUE BLUR...
HOW CAN YOU BEAM A BAT IN THE BLINK OF AN EYE?
WOOSH!
WOOSH!
WITH A BEAM OF LIGHT?

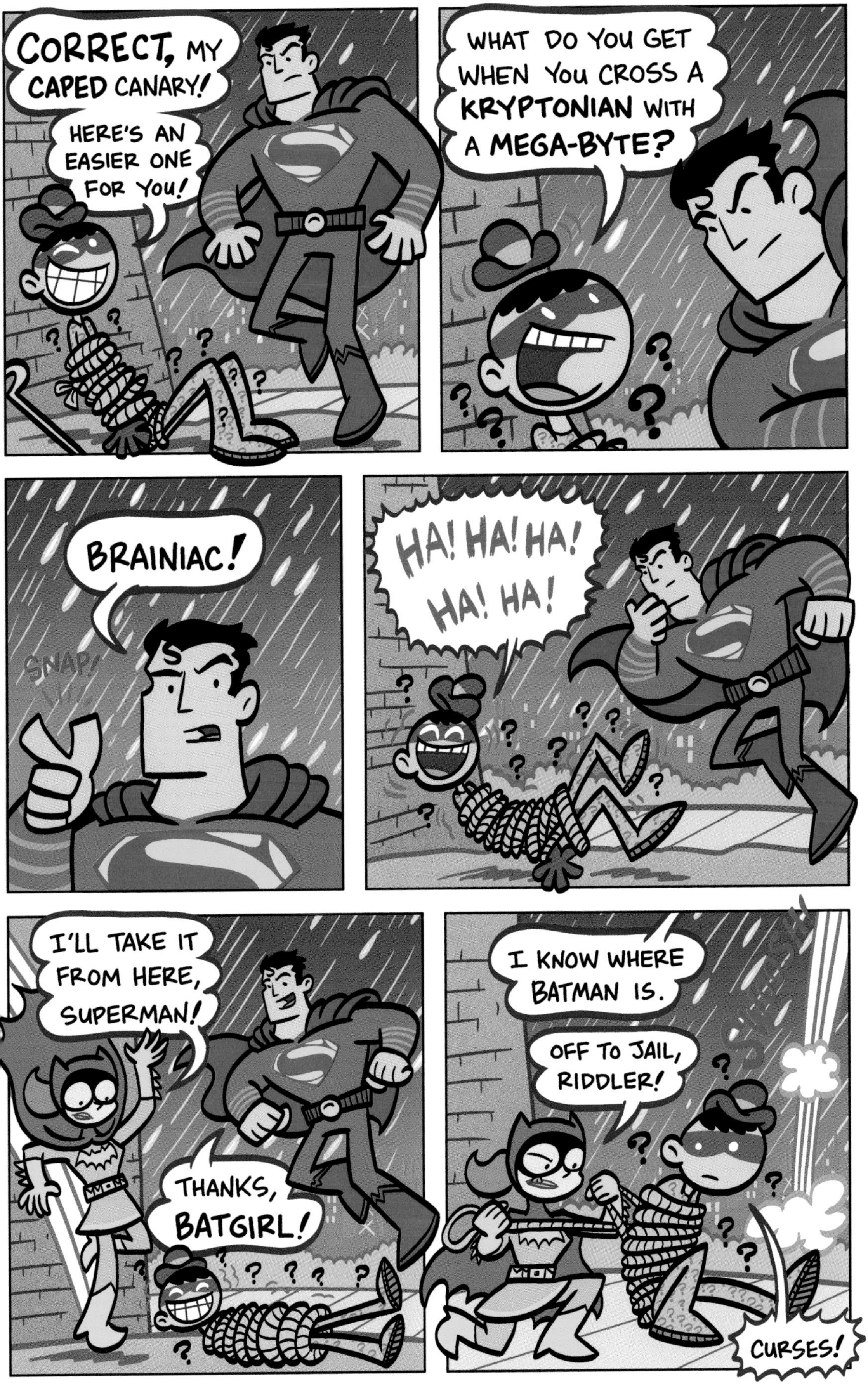
CORRECT, MY CAPED CANARY!
HERE'S AN EASIER ONE FOR YOU!
WHAT DO YOU GET WHEN YOU CROSS A KRYPTONIAN WITH A MEGA-BYTE?
BRAINIAC!
SNAP!
HA! HA! HA! HA! HA!
I'LL TAKE IT FROM HERE, SUPERMAN!
THANKS, BATGIRL!
I KNOW WHERE BATMAN IS.
OFF TO JAIL, RIDDLER!
CURSES!

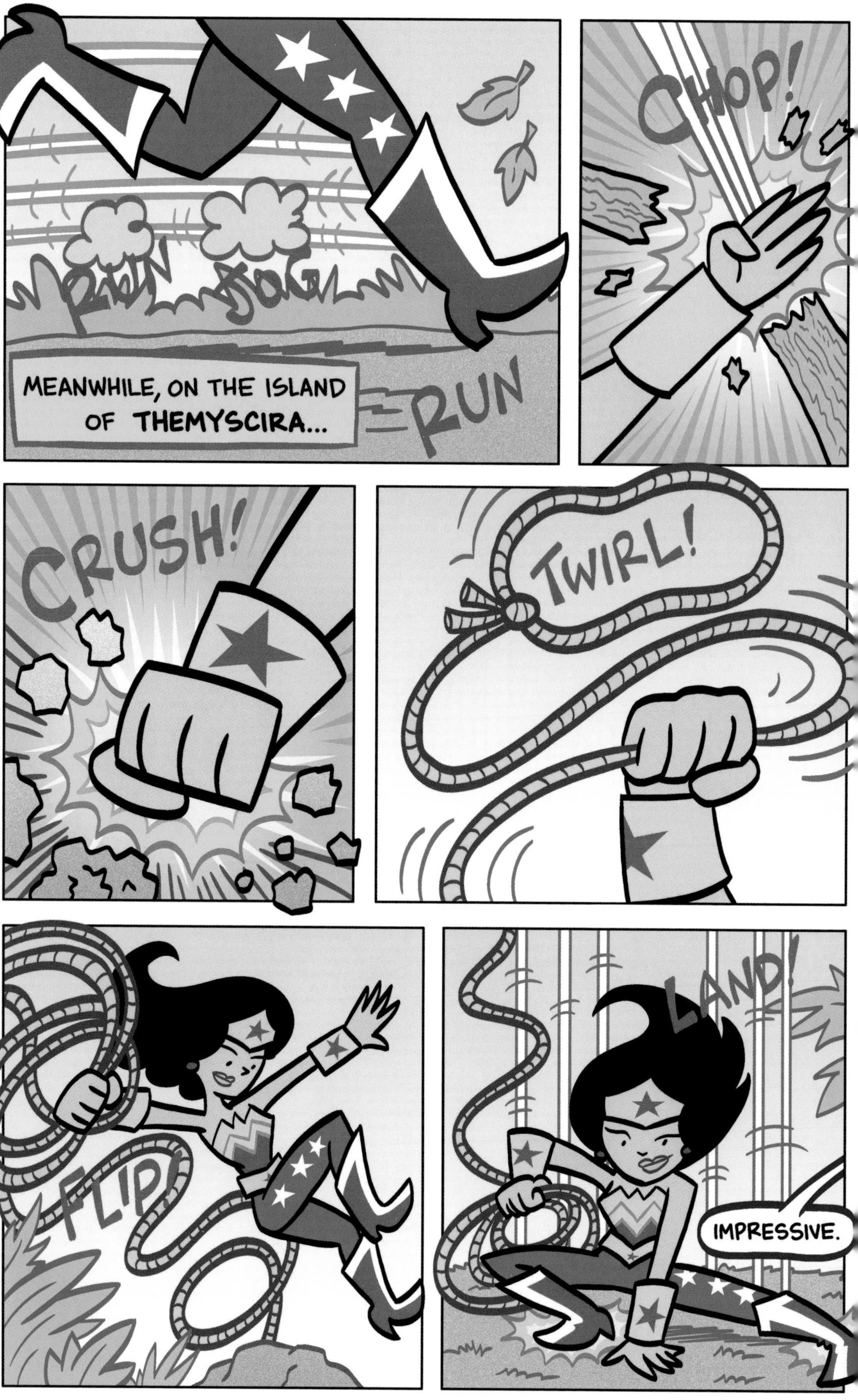

RUN
JOG
MEANWHILE, ON THE ISLAND OF THEMYSCIRA...
RUN
CHOP!
CRUSH!
TWIRL!
FLIP!
LAND!
IMPRESSIVE.

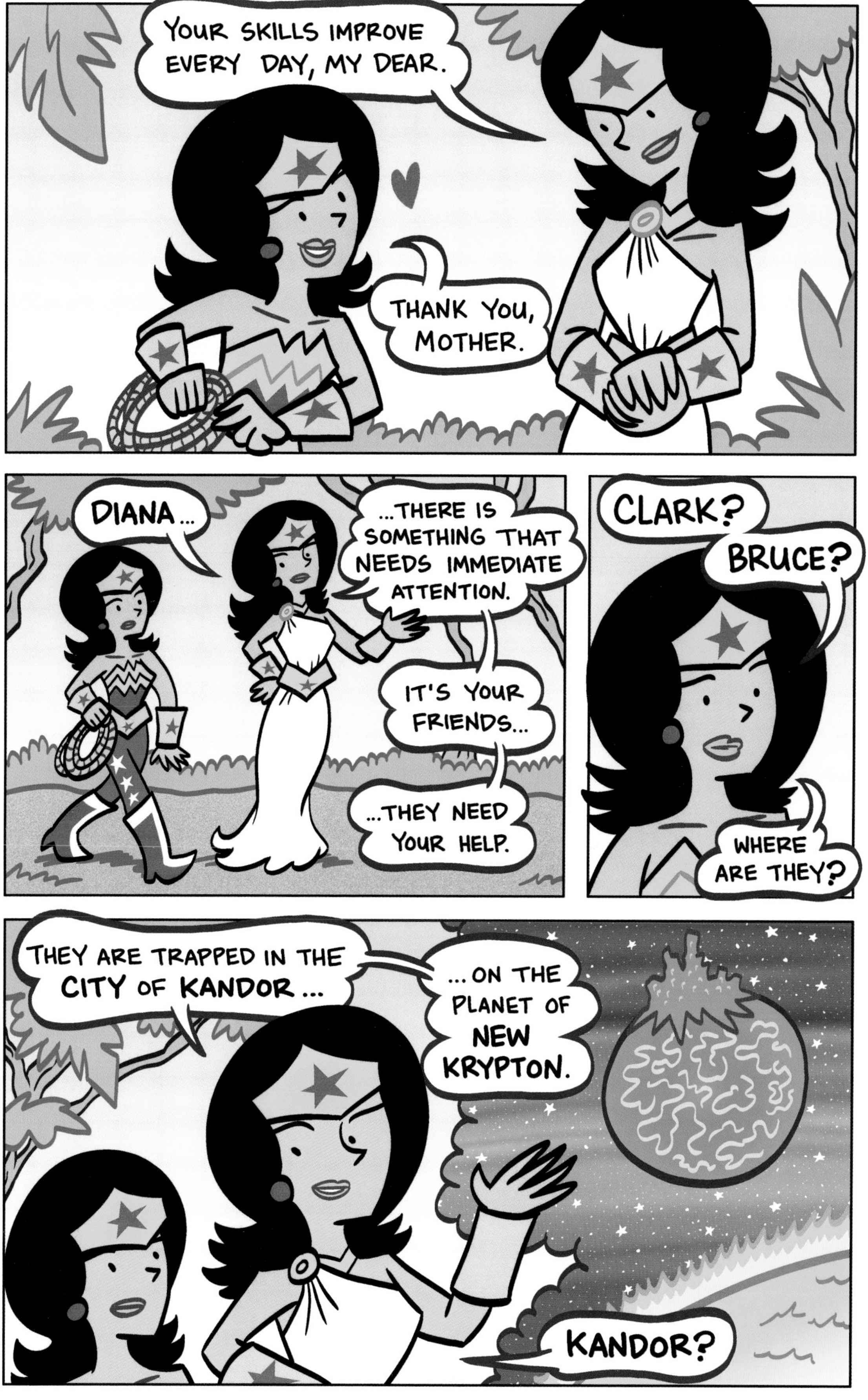

YOUR SKILLS IMPROVE EVERY DAY, MY DEAR.
THANK YOU, MOTHER.
DIANA...
...THERE IS SOMETHING THAT NEEDS IMMEDIATE ATTENTION.
IT'S YOUR FRIENDS...
...THEY NEED YOUR HELP.
CLARK?
BRUCE?
WHERE ARE THEY?
THEY ARE TRAPPED IN THE CITY OF KANDOR...
...ON THE PLANET OF NEW KRYPTON.
KANDOR?

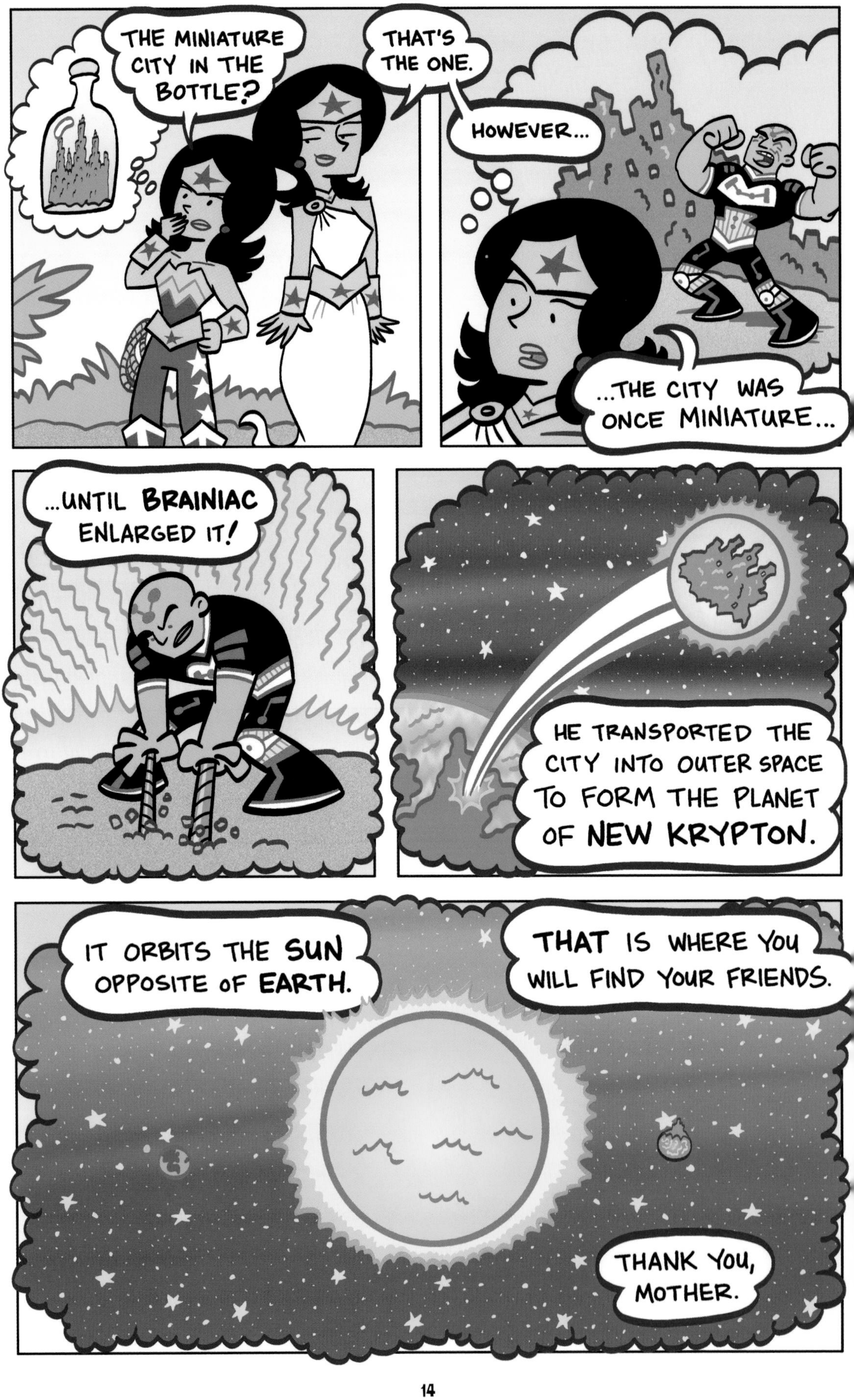
THE MINIATURE CITY IN THE BOTTLE?
THAT'S THE ONE.
HOWEVER...
...THE CITY WAS ONCE MINIATURE...
...UNTIL BRAINIAC ENLARGED IT!
HE TRANSPORTED THE CITY INTO OUTER SPACE TO FORM THE PLANET OF NEW KRYPTON.
IT ORBITS THE SUN OPPOSITE OF EARTH.
THAT IS WHERE YOU WILL FIND YOUR FRIENDS.
THANK YOU, MOTHER.

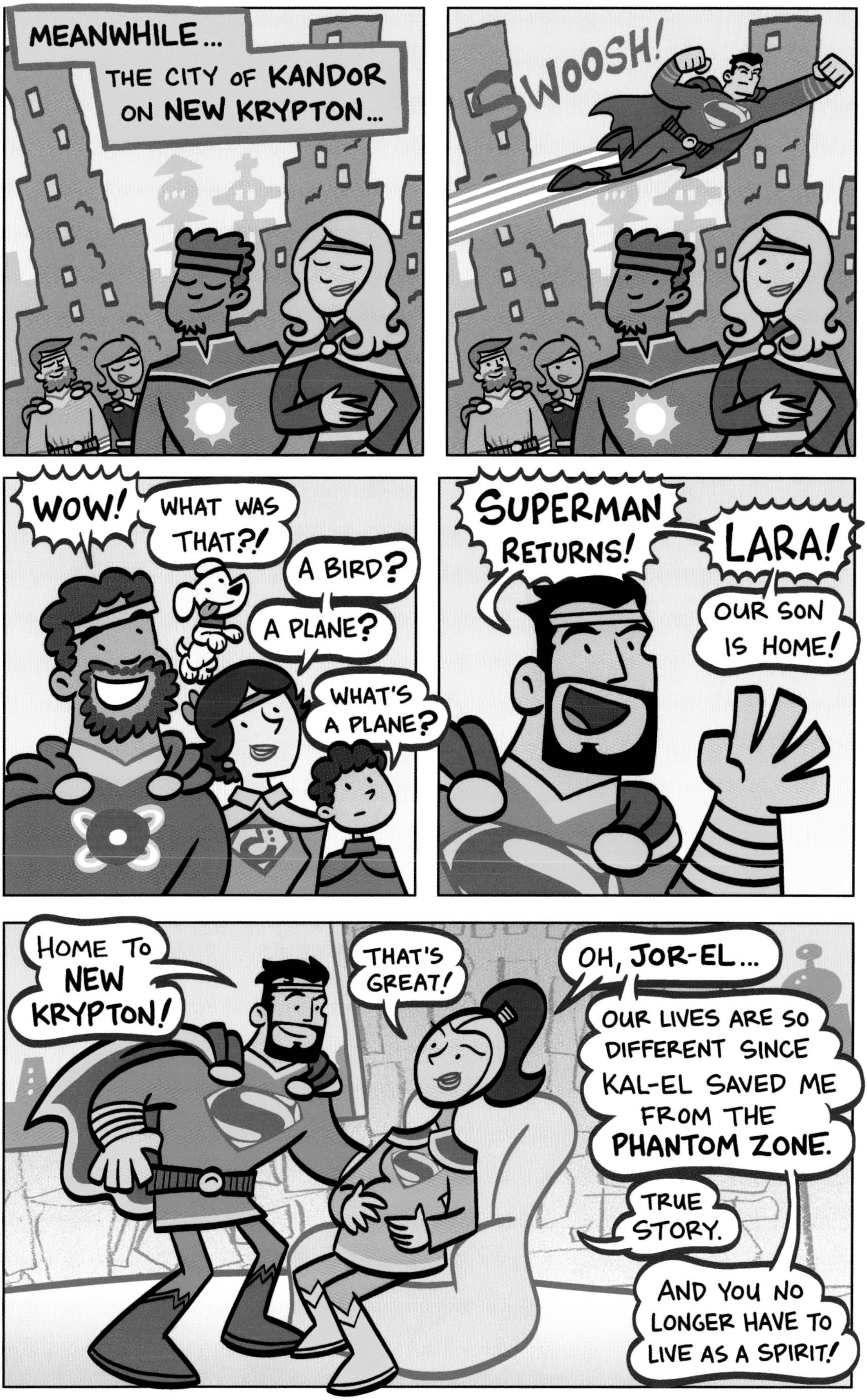
MEANWHILE...
THE CITY OF KANDOR ON NEW KRYPTON...
SWOOSH!
WOW!
WHAT WAS THAT?!
A BIRD?
A PLANE?
WHAT'S A PLANE?
SUPERMAN RETURNS!
LARA!
OUR SON IS HOME!
HOME TO NEW KRYPTON!
THAT'S GREAT!
OH, JOR-EL...
OUR LIVES ARE SO DIFFERENT SINCE KAL-EL SAVED ME FROM THE PHANTOM ZONE.
TRUE STORY.
AND YOU NO LONGER HAVE TO LIVE AS A SPIRIT!

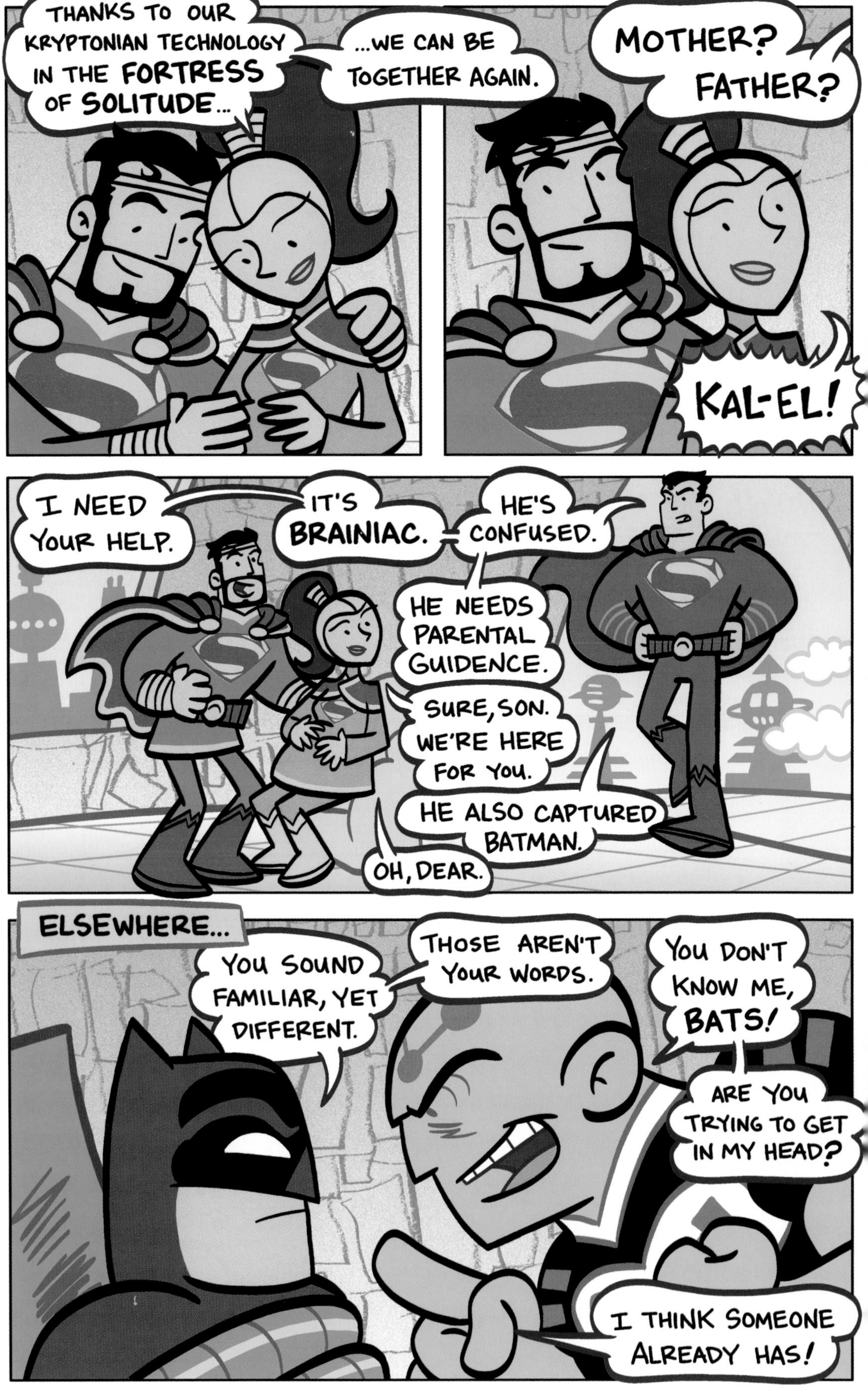
THANKS TO OUR KRYPTONIAN TECHNOLOGY IN THE FORTRESS OF SOLITUDE...
...WE CAN BE TOGETHER AGAIN.
MOTHER? FATHER?
KAL-EL!
I NEED YOUR HELP.
IT'S BRAINIAC.
HE'S CONFUSED.
HE NEEDS PARENTAL GUIDENCE.
SURE, SON. WE'RE HERE FOR YOU.
HE ALSO CAPTURED BATMAN.
OH, DEAR.
ELSEWHERE...
YOU SOUND FAMILIAR, YET DIFFERENT.
THOSE AREN'T YOUR WORDS.
YOU DON'T KNOW ME, BATS!
ARE YOU TRYING TO GET IN MY HEAD?
I THINK SOMEONE ALREADY HAS!

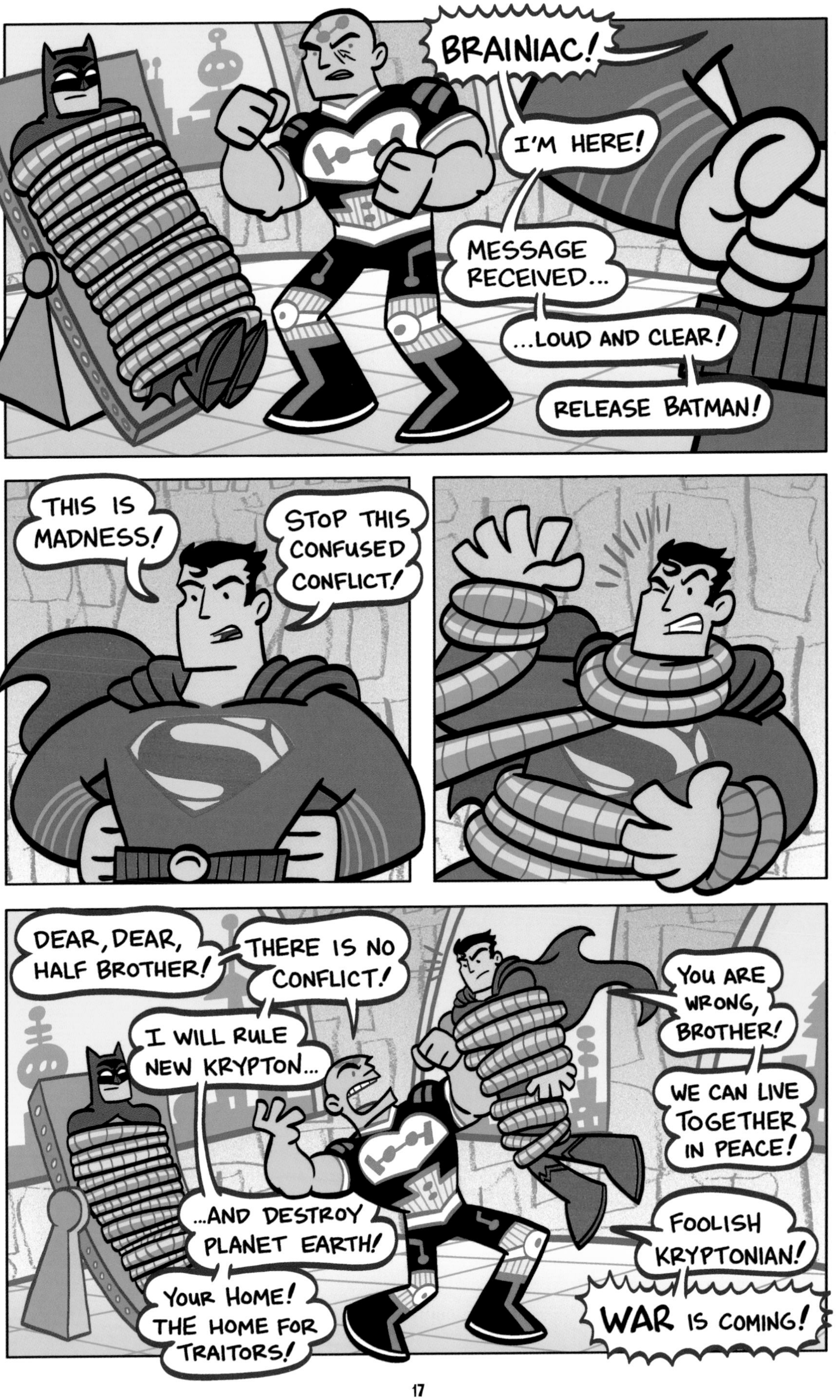
BRAINIAC!
I'M HERE!
MESSAGE RECEIVED...
...LOUD AND CLEAR!
RELEASE BATMAN!
THIS IS MADNESS!
STOP THIS CONFUSED CONFLICT!
DEAR, DEAR, HALF BROTHER!
THERE IS NO CONFLICT!
I WILL RULE NEW KRYPTON...
...AND DESTROY PLANET EARTH!
YOUR HOME! THE HOME FOR TRAITORS!
YOU ARE WRONG, BROTHER!
WE CAN LIVE TOGETHER IN PEACE!
FOOLISH KRYPTONIAN!
WAR IS COMING!

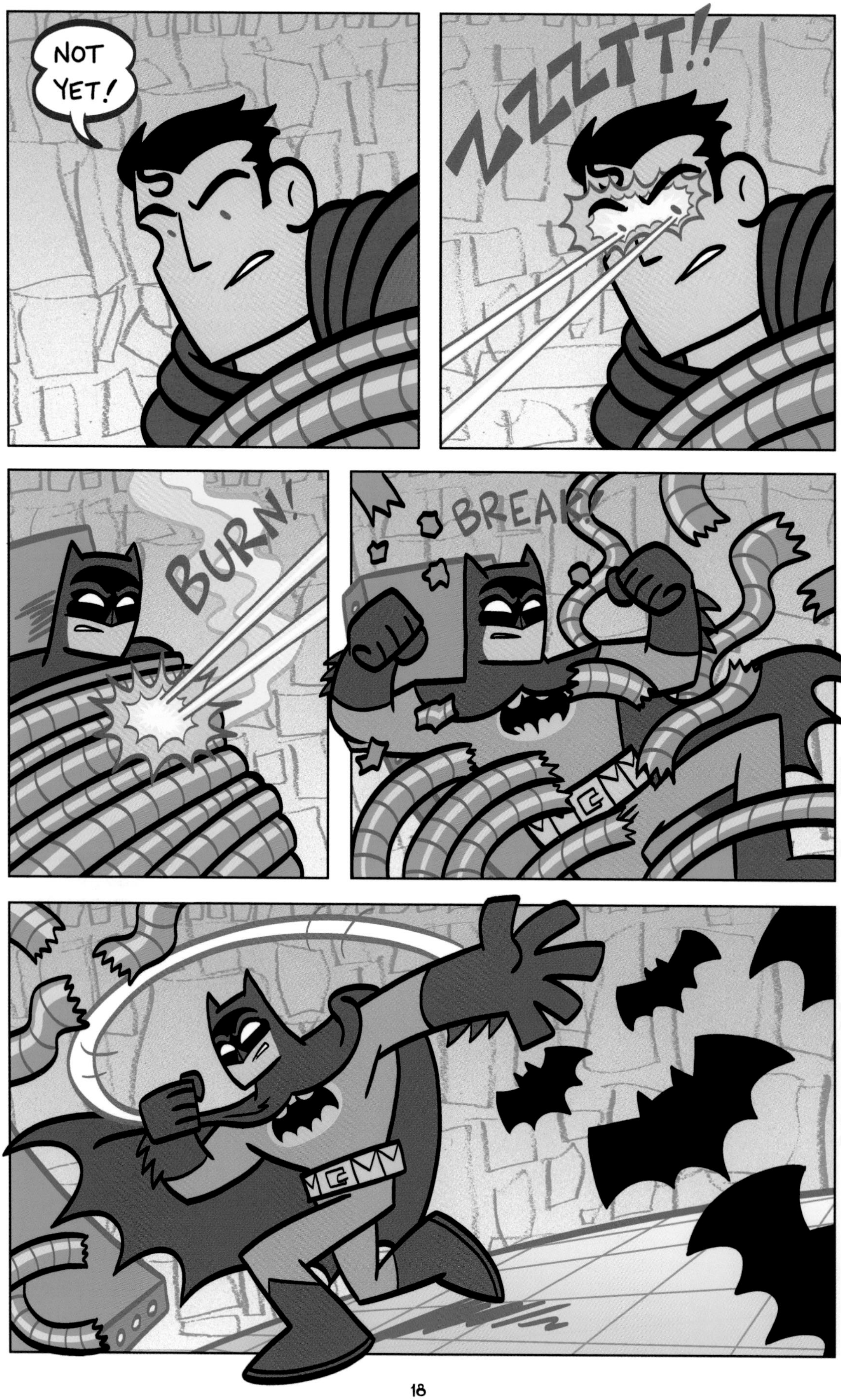
NOT YET!
ZZZZTT!!
BURN!
BREAK!

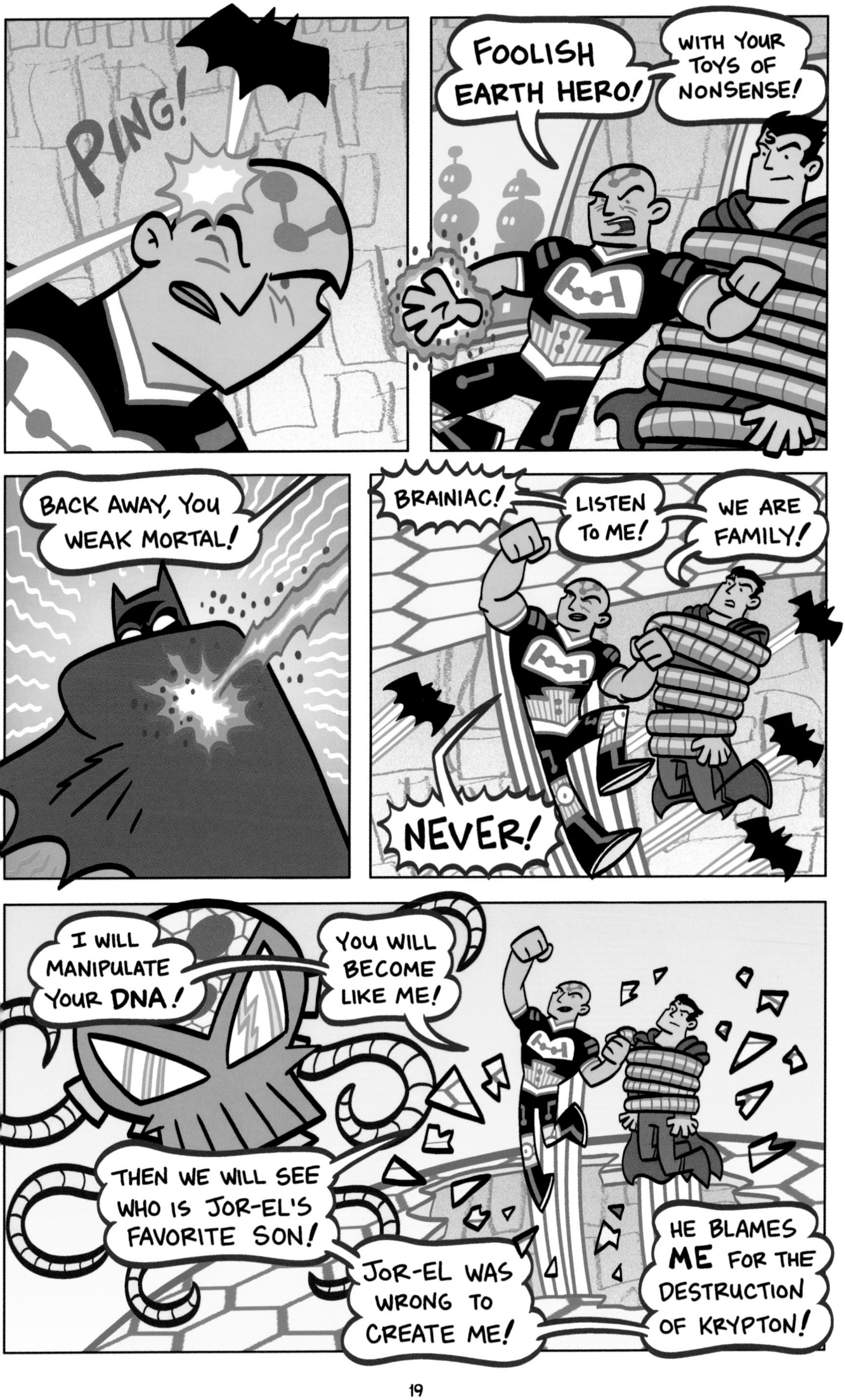
PING!
FOOLISH EARTH HERO!
WITH YOUR TOYS OF NONSENSE!
BACK AWAY, YOU WEAK MORTAL!
BRAINIAC!
LISTEN TO ME!
WE ARE FAMILY!
NEVER!
I WILL MANIPULATE YOUR DNA!
YOU WILL BECOME LIKE ME!
THEN WE WILL SEE WHO IS JOR-EL'S FAVORITE SON!
JOR-EL WAS WRONG TO CREATE ME!
HE BLAMES ME FOR THE DESTRUCTION OF KRYPTON!

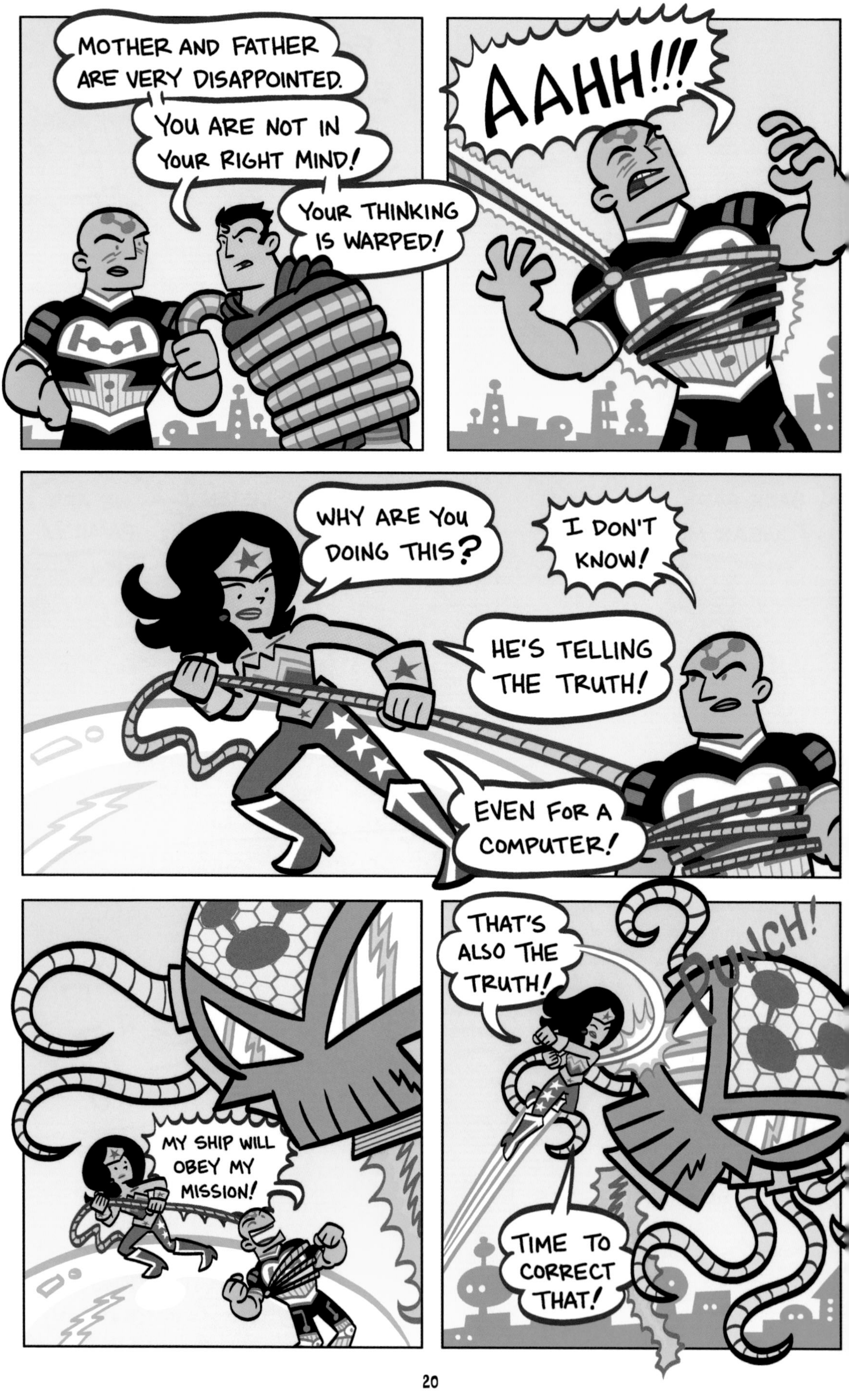
MOTHER AND FATHER ARE VERY DISAPPOINTED.
YOU ARE NOT IN YOUR RIGHT MIND!
YOUR THINKING IS WARPED!
AAHH!!!
WHY ARE YOU DOING THIS?
I DON'T KNOW!
HE'S TELLING THE TRUTH!
EVEN FOR A COMPUTER!
MY SHIP WILL OBEY MY MISSION!
THAT'S ALSO THE TRUTH!
PUNCH!
TIME TO CORRECT THAT!

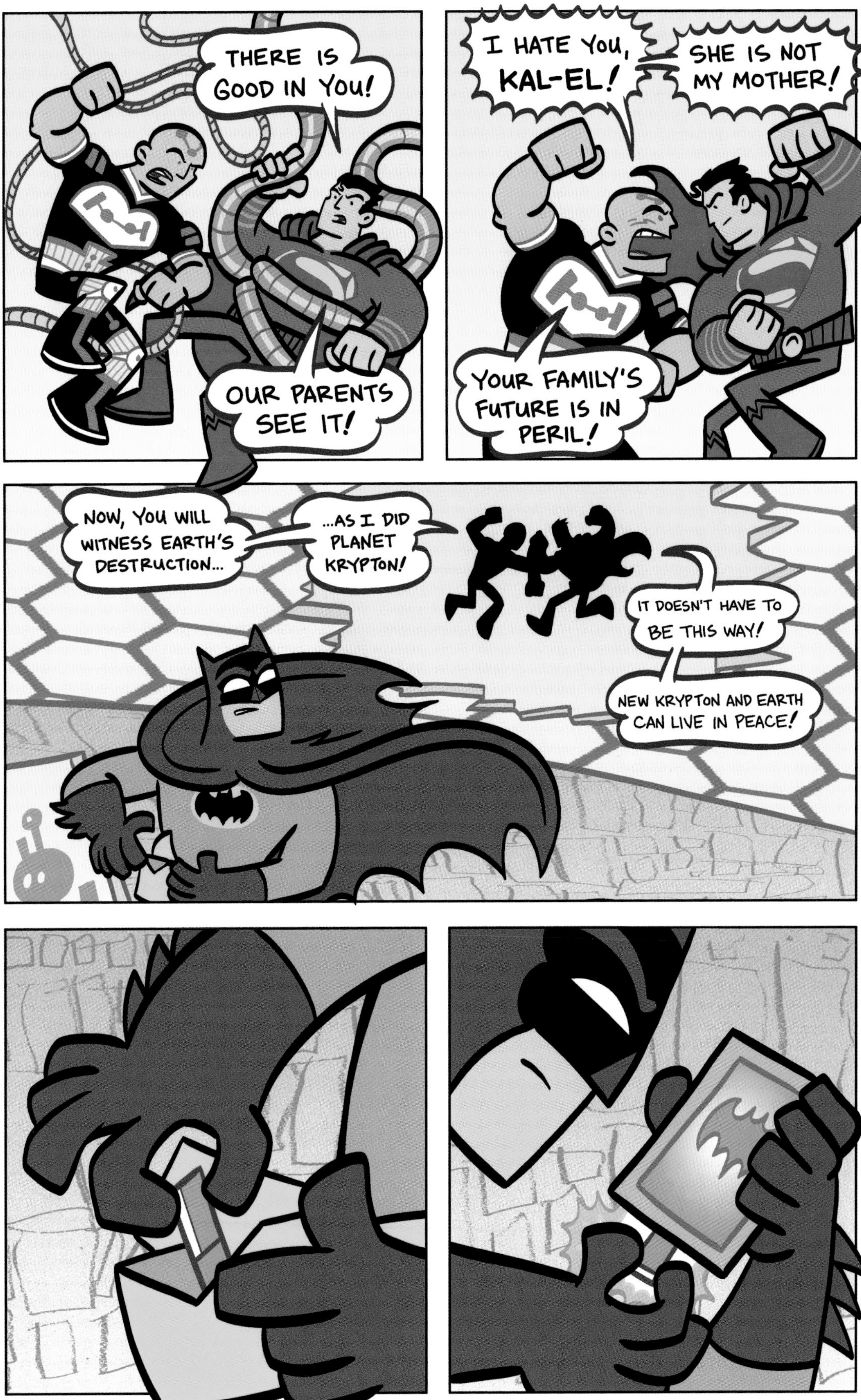
THERE IS GOOD IN YOU!
OUR PARENTS SEE IT!
I HATE YOU, KAL-EL!
SHE IS NOT MY MOTHER!
YOUR FAMILY'S FUTURE IS IN PERIL!
NOW, YOU WILL WITNESS EARTH'S DESTRUCTION...
...AS I DID PLANET KRYPTON!
IT DOESN'T HAVE TO BE THIS WAY!
NEW KRYPTON AND EARTH CAN LIVE IN PEACE!

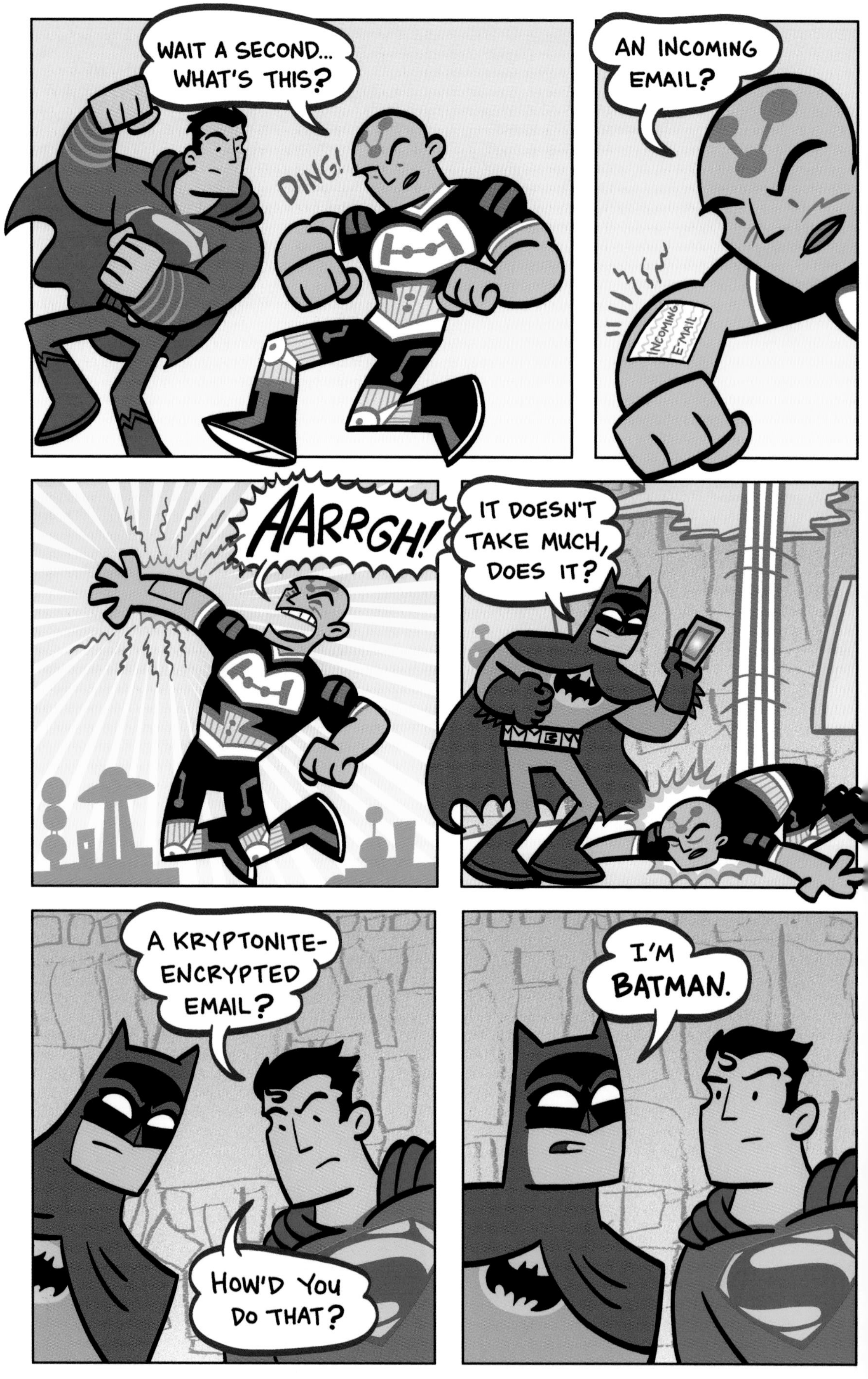

WAIT A SECOND... WHAT'S THIS?
DING!
AN INCOMING EMAIL?
INCOMING E-MAIL
AARRGH!
IT DOESN'T TAKE MUCH, DOES IT?
A KRYPTONITE-ENCRYPTED EMAIL?
HOW'D YOU DO THAT?
I'M BATMAN.

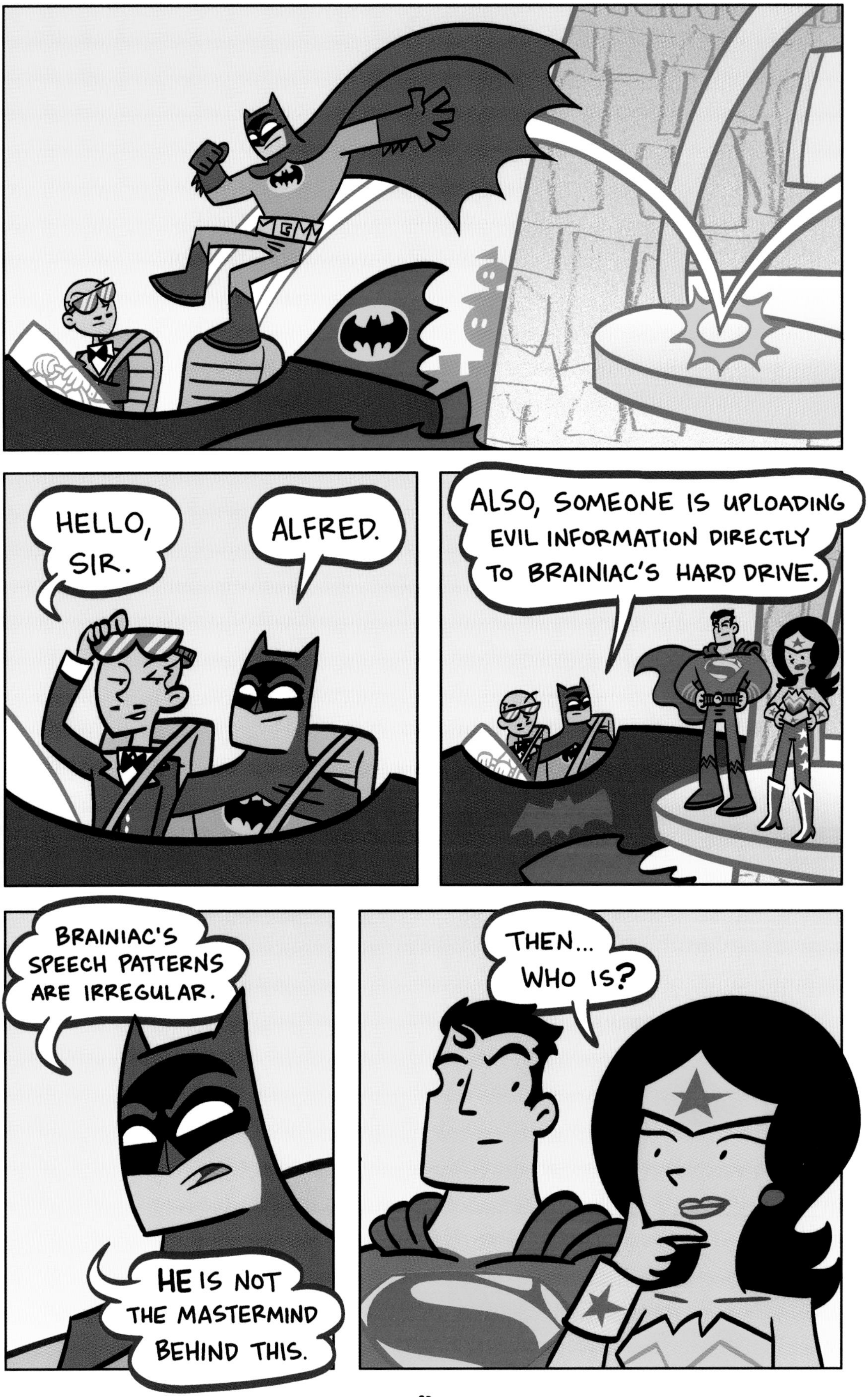
HELLO, SIR.
ALFRED.
ALSO, SOMEONE IS UPLOADING EVIL INFORMATION DIRECTLY TO BRAINIAC'S HARD DRIVE.
BRAINIAC'S SPEECH PATTERNS ARE IRREGULAR.
HE IS NOT THE MASTERMIND BEHIND THIS.
THEN... WHO IS?

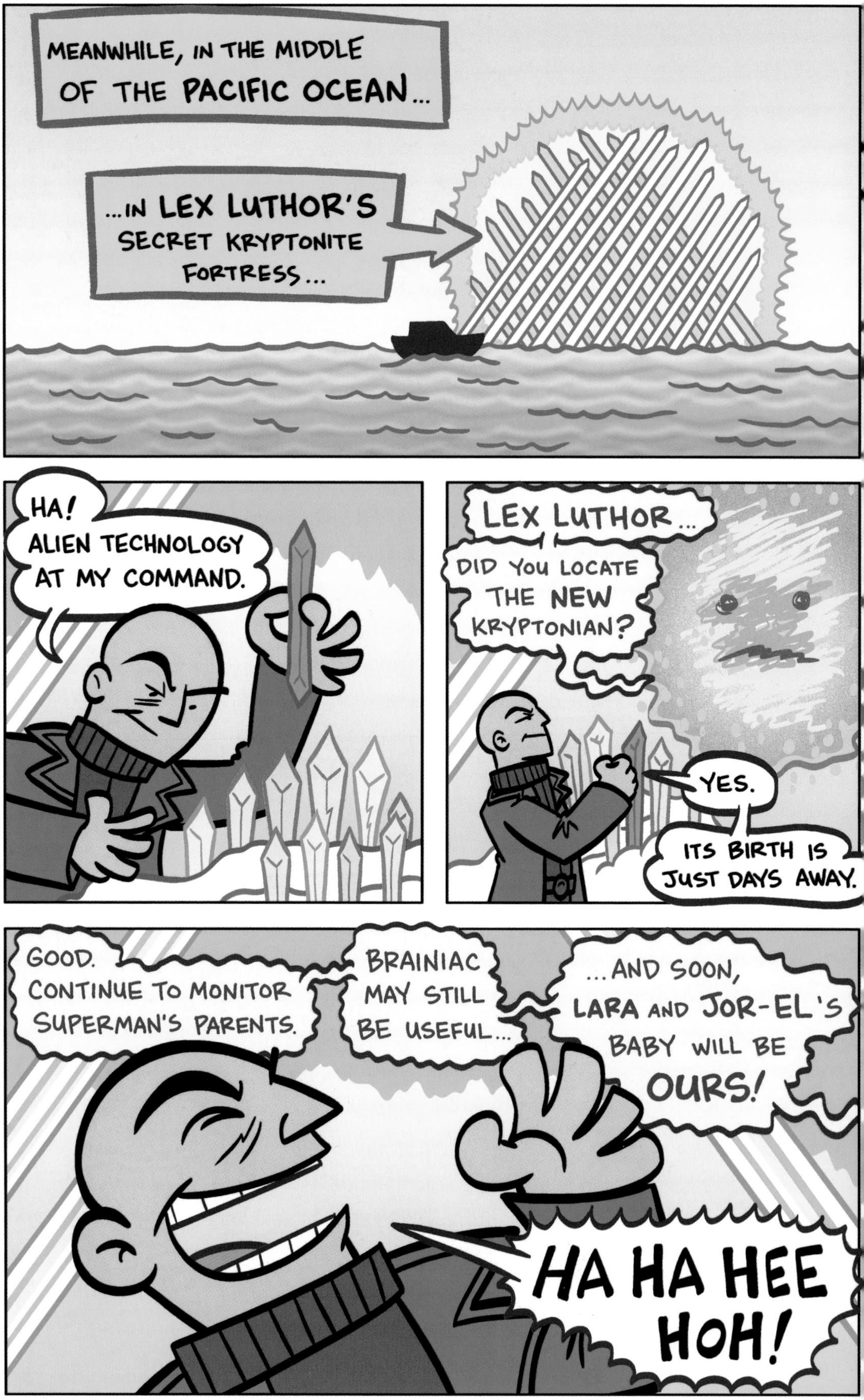
MEANWHILE, IN THE MIDDLE OF THE PACIFIC OCEAN...
...IN LEX LUTHOR'S SECRET KRYPTONITE FORTRESS...
HA! ALIEN TECHNOLOGY AT MY COMMAND.
LEX LUTHOR...
DID YOU LOCATE THE NEW KRYPTONIAN?
YES.
ITS BIRTH IS JUST DAYS AWAY.
GOOD. CONTINUE TO MONITOR SUPERMAN'S PARENTS.
BRAINIAC MAY STILL BE USEFUL...
...AND SOON, LARA AND JOR-EL'S BABY WILL BE OURS!
HA HA HEE HOH!

—WHO'S GONNA SAVE ME?

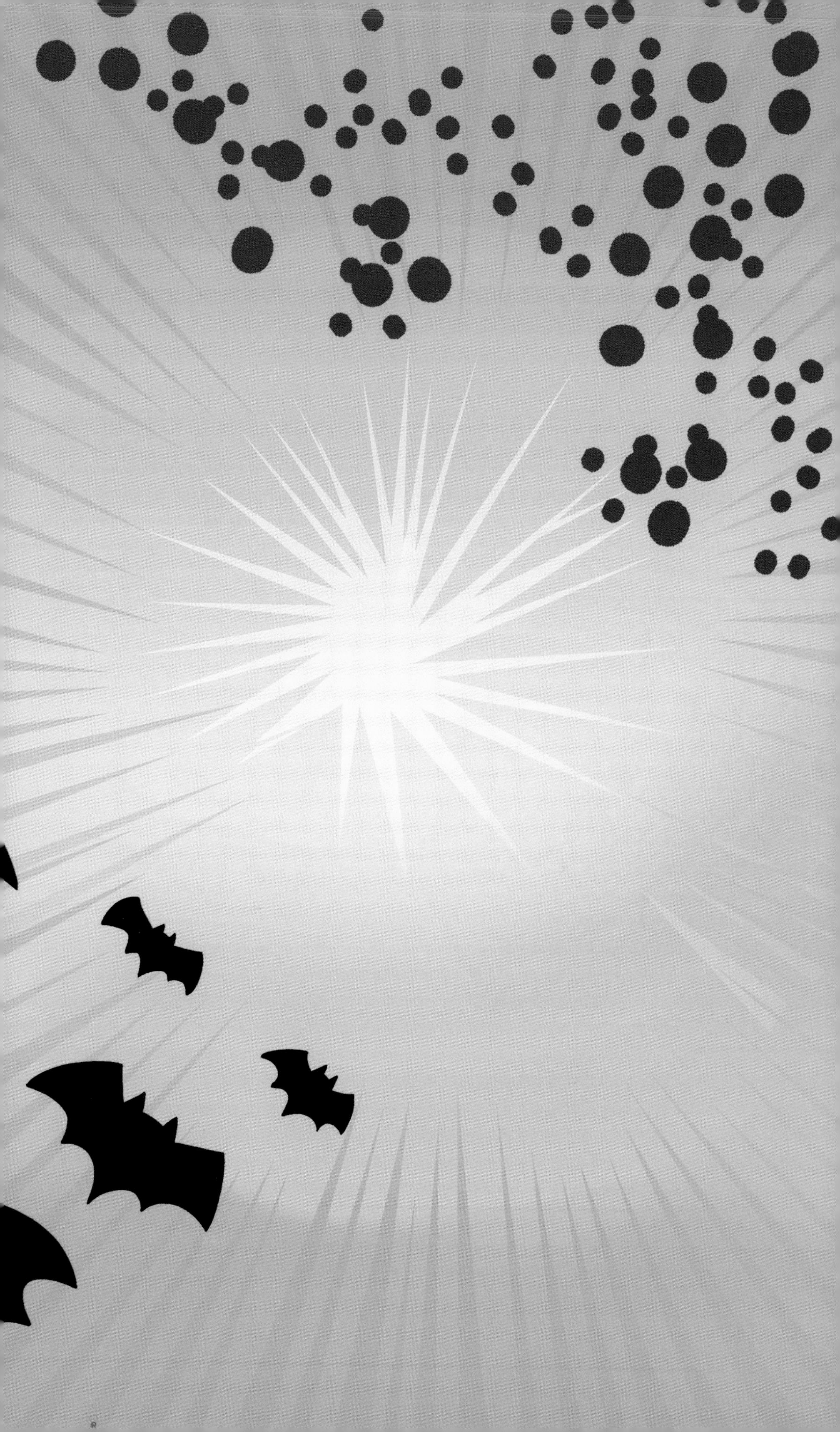

CREATORS

ART BALTAZAR IS A CARTOONIST MACHINE FROM THE HEART OF CHICAGO! HE DEFINES CARTOONS AND COMICS NOT ONLY AS AN ART STYLE, BUT AS A WAY OF LIFE. CURRENTLY, ART IS THE CREATIVE FORCE BEHIND *THE NEW YORK TIMES* BEST-SELLING, EISNER AWARD-WINNING DC COMICS SERIES TINY TITANS, THE CO-WRITER FOR *BILLY BATSON AND THE MAGIC OF SHAZAM!,* AND CO-CREATOR OF SUPERMAN FAMILY ADVENTURES. ART IS LIVING THE DREAM! HE DRAWS COMICS AND NEVER HAS TO LEAVE THE HOUSE. HE LIVES WITH HIS LOVELY WIFE, ROSE, BIG BOY SONNY, LITTLE BOY GORDON, AND LITTLE GIRL AUDREY. RIGHT ON!

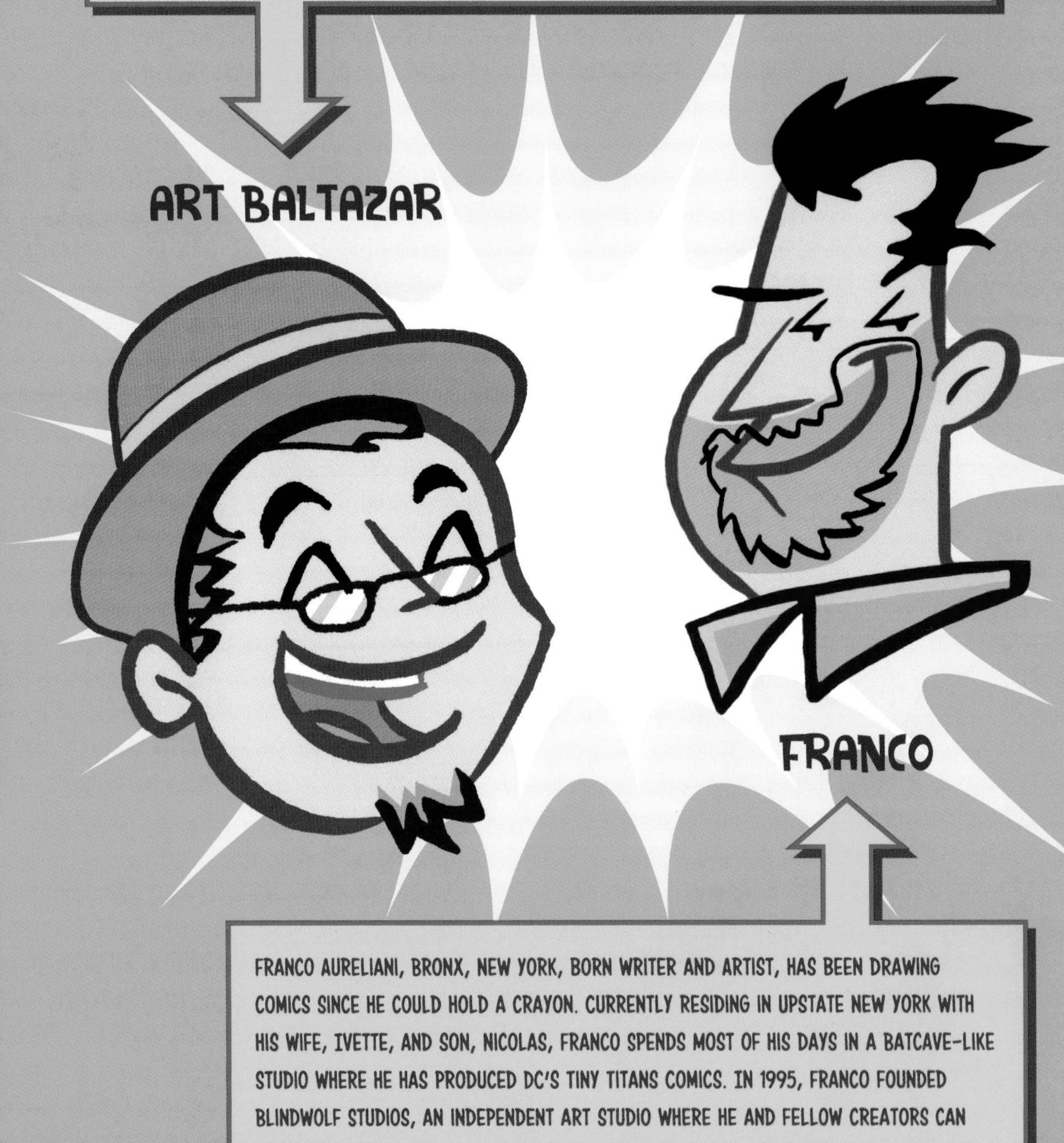
ART BALTAZAR
FRANCO

FRANCO AURELIANI, BRONX, NEW YORK, BORN WRITER AND ARTIST, HAS BEEN DRAWING COMICS SINCE HE COULD HOLD A CRAYON. CURRENTLY RESIDING IN UPSTATE NEW YORK WITH HIS WIFE, IVETTE, AND SON, NICOLAS, FRANCO SPENDS MOST OF HIS DAYS IN A BATCAVE-LIKE STUDIO WHERE HE HAS PRODUCED DC'S TINY TITANS COMICS. IN 1995, FRANCO FOUNDED BLINDWOLF STUDIOS, AN INDEPENDENT ART STUDIO WHERE HE AND FELLOW CREATORS CAN CREATE CHILDREN'S COMICS. FRANCO IS THE CREATOR, ARTIST, AND WRITER OF *PATRICK THE WOLF BOY*. WHEN HE'S NOT WRITING AND DRAWING, FRANCO ALSO TEACHES HIGH SCHOOL ART.

GLOSSARY

delusional (duh-LOO-zhuhn-al)—to be mistaken, or have misleading beliefs

destruction (di-STRUHK-shuhn)—what happens when something is destroyed

DNA (dee-en-AY)—material in cells that gives people their individual characteristics; DNA stands for deoxyribonucleic acid

encrypted (in-KRIP-tid)—when information has been hidden with a secret code or cypher

enlarge (in-LARJ)—to make something bigger

fortress (FOR-triss)—a building or place that is strengthened against attack

lure (LOO-uhr)—to draw something in with a fake reward

manipulate (muh-NIP-yuh-late)—to change something in a clever way to influence people to do or think how you want

mastermind (MASS-tur-minde)—the main planner, or the original source of a plot

miniature (MIN-ee-uh-choor)—much smaller than usual size

peril (PER-uhl)—danger; something dangerous

solitude (SAH-luh-tood)—to be alone

technology (tek-NOL-uh-jee)—the use of science to do practical things, such as designing complex machines

traitor (TRAY-tur)—someone who aids the enemy of their allies or country

warped (WORPD)—something becoming bent or twisted over time

witness (WIT-niss)—a person who has seen or heard something

VISUAL QUESTIONS AND WRITING PROMPTS

1. REREAD PAGES 10 AND 11 AGAIN. WHY DO YOU THINK THE RIDDLER HELPS SUPERMAN IN THESE PANELS?

CORRECT, MY CAPED CANARY!
HERE'S AN EASIER ONE FOR YOU!
1
WHAT DO YOU GET WHEN YOU CROSS A KRYPTONIAN WITH A MEGA-BYTE?

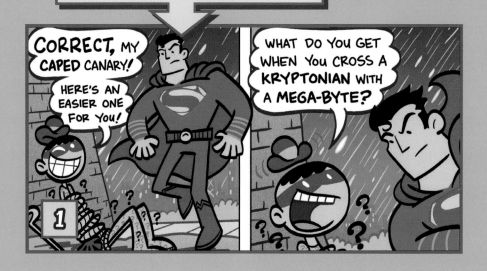

2. LOOK AT THE FACIAL EXPRESSIONS BELOW. WHAT DO THEY TELL YOU ABOUT LIFE ON NEW KRYPTON?

MEANWHILE...
THE CITY OF KANDOR ON NEW KRYPTON...
2
SWOOSH!

3. IMAGINE SUPERMAN'S PARENTS TALK TO BRAINIAC AFTER THE EVENTS IN THIS BOOK. WRITE DOWN THEIR CONVERSATION.

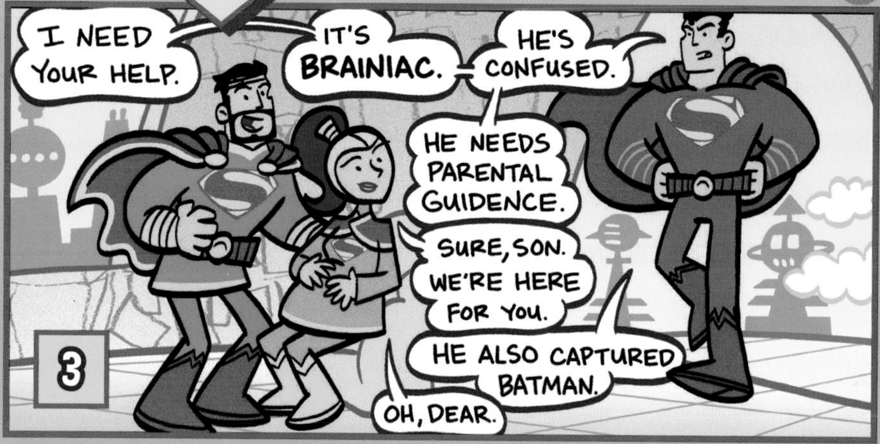

3
I NEED YOUR HELP.
IT'S BRAINIAC.
HE'S CONFUSED.
HE NEEDS PARENTAL GUIDENCE.
SURE, SON. WE'RE HERE FOR YOU.
HE ALSO CAPTURED BATMAN.
OH, DEAR.

4. BRAINIAC IS SUPERMAN'S HALF BROTHER IN THIS STORY. WHAT SIMILARITIES CAN YOU SEE BETWEEN THE TWO? WHAT DIFFERENCES?

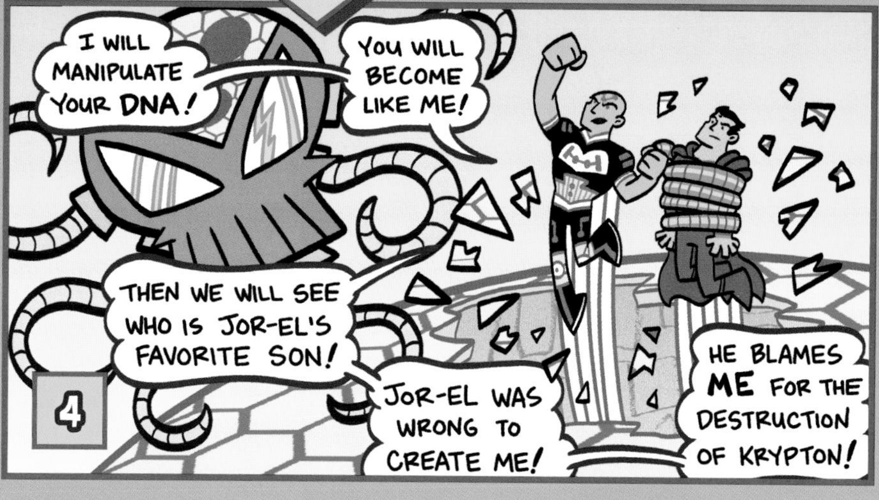

4
I WILL MANIPULATE YOUR DNA!
YOU WILL BECOME LIKE ME!
THEN WE WILL SEE WHO IS JOR-EL'S FAVORITE SON!
JOR-EL WAS WRONG TO CREATE ME!
HE BLAMES ME FOR THE DESTRUCTION OF KRYPTON!

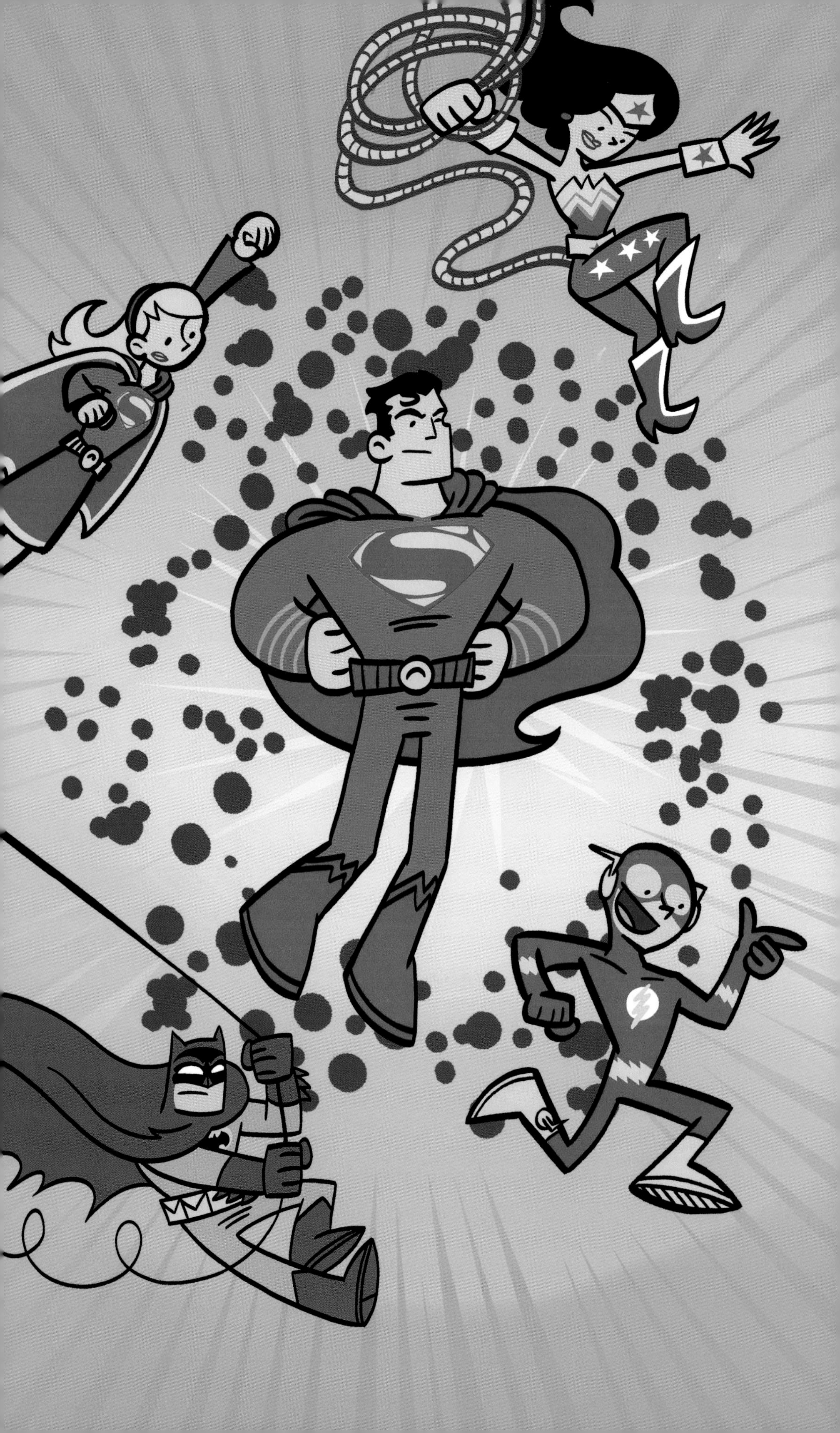

READ THEM ALL!

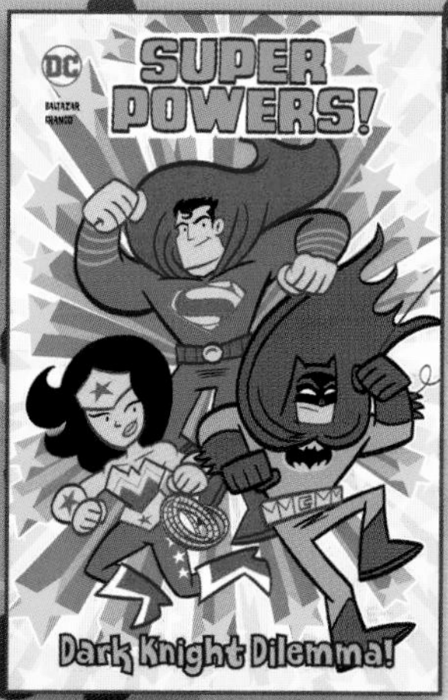
SUPER POWERS!
Dark Knight Dilemma!

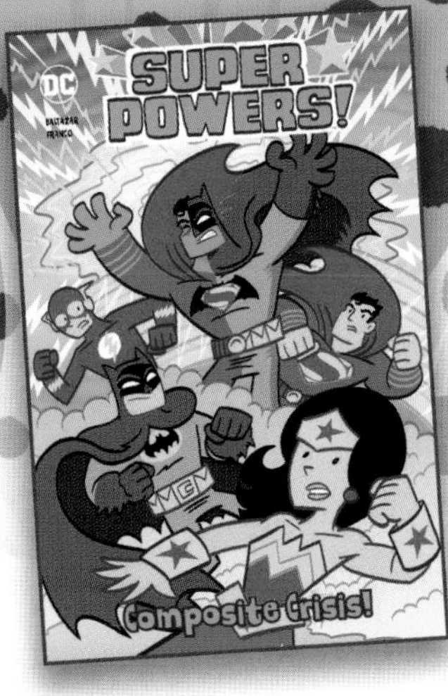
SUPER POWERS!
Composite Crisis!

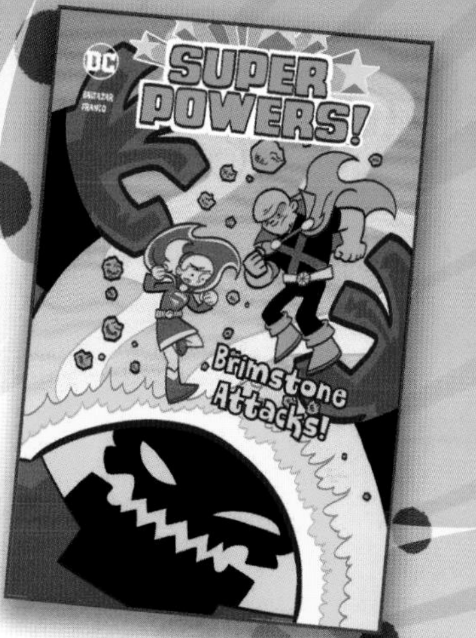
SUPER POWERS!
Brimstone Attacks!

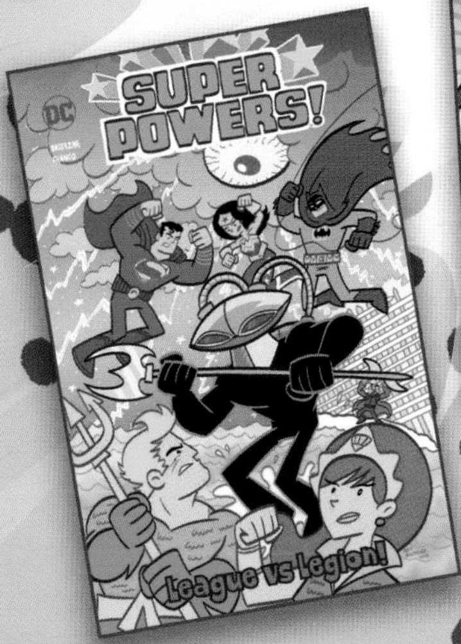
SUPER POWERS!
League vs Legion!

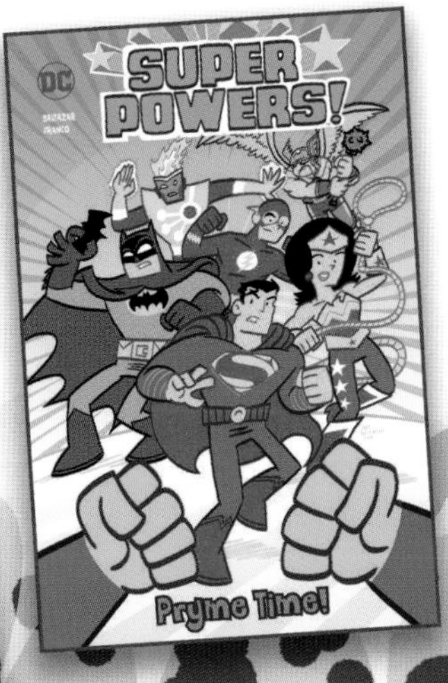
SUPER POWERS!
Pryme Time!

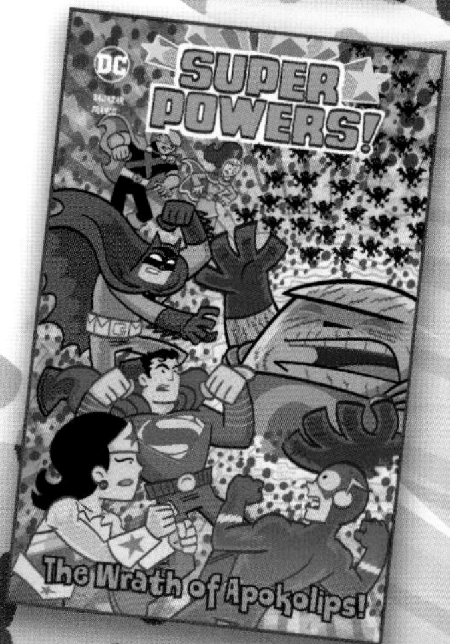
SUPER POWERS!
The Wrath of Apokolips!

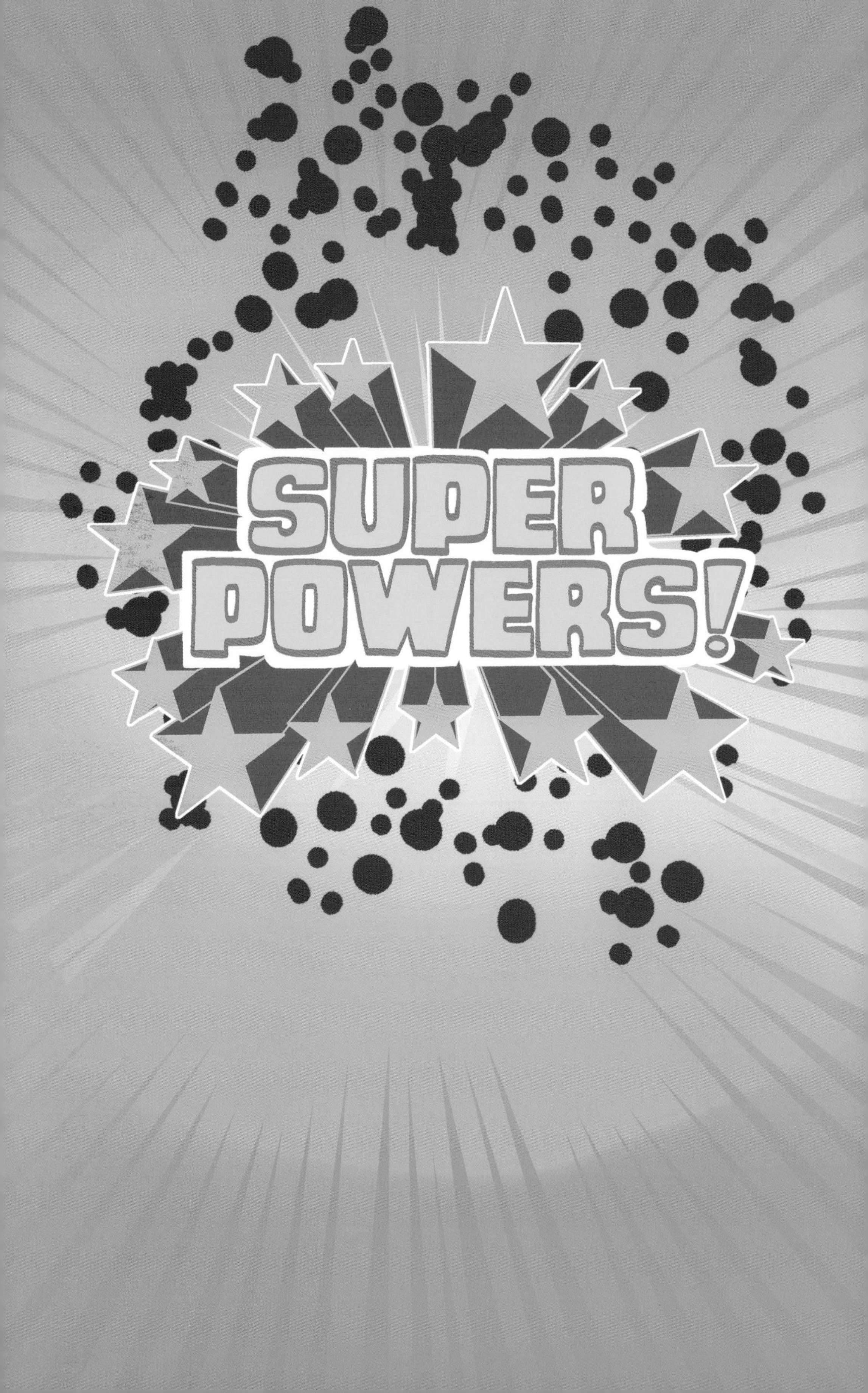
SUPER
POWERS!